Mr Darcy's Christmas Carol: A Pride and Prejudice Variation

Meg Osborne

Published by Meg Osborne, 2017.

This is a work of fiction. Similarities to real people, places, or events are entirely coincidental.

MR DARCY'S CHRISTMAS CAROL: A PRIDE AND PREJUDICE VARIATION

First edition. November 20, 2017.

Copyright © 2017 Meg Osborne.

ISBN: 1979917213

Written by Meg Osborne.

Also by Meg Osborne

A Convenient Marriage
Longbourn's Lark: A Pride and Prejudice Variation
Three Weeks in Kent: A Pride and Prejudice Variation
Suitably Wed: A Pride and Prejudice Variation

Fate and Fortune
Too Fond of Stars: A Persuasion Variation
A Temporary Peace: A Persuasion Variation

Love Remains
Reacquainted
Rediscovered
Reunited
Love Remains Omnibus

Pathway to Pemberley

The Collins Conundrum: A Pride and Prejudice Variation
The Wickham Wager: A Pride and Prejudice Variation
The Darcy Decision: A Pride and Prejudice Variation

Standalone

After the Letter: A Persuasion Continuation
Half the Sum of Attraction: A Persuasion Prequel
A Very Merry Masquerade: A Pride and Prejudice Variation Novella
The Other Elizabeth Bennet: A Pride and Prejudice Variation Novella
In Netherfield Library and Other Stories
Mr Darcy's Christmas Carol: A Pride and Prejudice Variation

Watch for more at www.megosbornewrites.com.

Chapter One

"Merry Christmas!"
"Season's greetings!"

Fitzwilliam Darcy plastered a polite smile onto his usually grim features. It cost him no small effort, and as a result, the expression was hardly convincing. He was not fond of London society, even when he did not also have Christmas to contend with.

As if sensing the irritable turn his thoughts had taken, Caroline Bingley appeared from within the crowd and greeted him with a dazzling grin that was almost disturbing in its enthusiasm.

"What a wonderful evening this has been," she declared, glancing around her as if the presence of several members of London's high society served only to emphasise her words. "It was a very good idea of yours, Mr Darcy, to return to London for Christmas. Just imagine how dreary Hertfordshire would have been at this time of year." A malicious gleam lit her eyes. "We might have been forced into attending an advent gathering at Longbourn, rather than an evening such as this."

This comment was engineered solely to garner a reaction, and Darcy was unable to prevent a reflexive grimace from settling over his features. An evening in a crowded London townhouse, marking the season among his colleagues and contemporaries might be scarcely bearable to him, but the thought of a noisy, crowded Christmas party at the home of Elizabeth Bennet was a painful prospect, even in imagination.

"Dreary is not the word I would have used," he remarked, fixing his gaze straight ahead, towards the exit, the route of escape he might take when polite obligation had been met, and he was at last permitted to leave.

Caroline laughed as if his words had been a joke. The noise grated on his nerves, and he recalled another young lady's laugh, at another social gathering he had been pressed into attending. His frown deepened, and he shook his head slightly to clear the memory. He had come to London, in part, to escape one Bennet sister. He certainly did not mean to cede his thoughts to the other at every opportunity.

"Where is your brother?" he asked, little caring if his tone were brusque. Where such a mood might offend or upset a young woman of more delicate disposition than Miss Caroline Bingley, even outright insult would not be enough to deter her interest in him. *Accompanying them to London at Caroline's suggestion hardly helped my cause*, he thought ruefully. *I did it for Charles.* Yet, now that they were all here, he wondered at the wisdom of the move.

"Charles?" Caroline shrugged her shoulders, affecting ignorance, although the way her eyes immediately sought out the fireplace betrayed her full and certain knowledge that Charles Bingley was precisely where she had left him, occupying a seat near the hearth and staring morosely into the embers. "I am sure he is quite content," she said, as if discussing her brother with Mr Darcy was the very last thing she wished to do at that precise moment. This served only to irritate Darcy further, for it was concerning Charles that she was forever seeking his attention. *It is only concerning Charles,* Darcy thought, *that I give her my attention to begin with.*

This was uncharitable, and he felt the disapproval that Georgiana would have given such a sentiment. Georgiana was not here, and Darcy had had his fill of the social manoeuvres of Miss Caroline Bingley long before that evening. She may have posed the question of London as being in Charles's best interests, pressing Darcy into service to separate Charles from a match neither of them approved of, but she certainly did not act entirely out of altruism. In fact, of the three of them, she seemed the only one content with their current position.

"Darcy!" Sir George Newton joined the duo with a booming laugh. "I thought I saw you lurking here in the corridor. You do not often grace us with your presence here at Christmas!"

"This year seems to be the exception," Darcy said, with a polite smile.

"Well, then you cannot mean to stay hiding all evening! I know you shall not wish to dance, and so I shall offer you escape before my dear lady wife ensnares you for her own ends. A group of us are settling to play a hand of whist: come and make a four."

If there was an excuse, Darcy could not find it, and so it was with resignation that he allowed Sir George to lead him away. It freed him from Caroline Bingley's unfettered attention, however, and for that must be rejoiced in. He liked Sir George, as well as he liked any of the London set, and the game occupied all four men in playing, rather than talking, so that the evening passed relatively pleasantly.

"Well, good evening, gentlemen," Darcy said, standing at the close of what would be his last hand. He had stayed longer than he had originally planned, and certainly long enough to be considered polite, yet even so he was not unhappy to be able to make his excuses and turn towards home. He scanned the crowd as he left, to see if he could make out Charles and Caroline. Mercifully, Caroline was fully occupied - this time in conversation with two other young ladies, evidently observing all around them and passing judgment as they saw fit. His friend was not in his usual seat by the fire, and at last, Darcy distinguished him, dancing with an elegant dark-haired young woman. He could see Charles' partner only from behind but something about her movements struck him as eminently familiar. She turned, then, and for half a moment Darcy recognised Elizabeth Bennet. He was shocked into stillness, wondering what on earth she was doing in London, and why Caroline stood idly by, enabling, if not encouraging, her brother to dance with the sister of the woman they had sought to remove from his circle. He blinked, and the young woman's features shifted She was not Elizabeth at all, but some other young woman, with softer features and a less determined chin. Darcy shook his head, wondering why his mind had chosen to play such a trick - and why, of all the women in his acquaintance, it chose to taunt him with Elizabeth Bennet's apparition. Swallowing his discomfort, he acknowledged that Charles, if not happy, was at least fully occupied in dancing. His sister would, Darcy hoped, see to it that her brother was forced into society more than he would choose in his current mood, and with greater success than Darcy would achieve.

He saw his chance, then, for an unhindered escape, and took it, hurrying out into the winter night without a backward glance, lest any other ghosts of Meryton attempted to assail him.

Usually, the proximity of one house to another was something Darcy disliked about London, but this evening he was glad it would be but a short walk back to his townhouse. He hurried down the street so quickly that he quite ignored several acquaintances, who paused to wish him the greetings of the season. He could not quite let go of the notion of Elizabeth Bennet appearing before his eyes, as if fate determined he would not forget her as easily as he intended. *It was a trick of the light and no more,* he reasoned, but even so, his anxiety did not completely recede, and he did not slow his pace until he reached his own door-step. There, with the door closed behind him and surrounded by his own familiar belongings, he might relax at last.

AFTER AN HOUR'S PEACE in his study, he had anticipated his anxieties receding. If anything, though, he found his thoughts straying to Hertfordshire even more.

"Too much society," he grumbled aloud. "And too much brandy." He reached for water, not wanting to agitate the kitchen staff in seeking something as soothing as milk. He was a grown man, not a boy in need of a comforting drink to chase away a bad dream. Even so, he shuddered, in spite of the warm fire blazing in the hearth, and pulled his favourite armchair a foot or two closer to the flames. The sound of London's night-time bustle began to fade from his notice and the comforting crackle of the fire, along with its warmth, began to lull him towards sleep. As his head nodded he wondered, drowsily, whether he ought to retire to bed.

His window, which had been left open to allow the tiniest crack of fresh air to circulate, suddenly caught on a breeze and pulled wide The gust of wind billowed the curtains momentarily, before slamming the glass shut with a finality that startled Darcy out of his half-sleep. His candles had been all but extinguished by the gust, and the noise of the window slamming closed again summoned his housekeeper, who knocked and entered, stifling a yawn.

"Are you alright, sir?" she asked, hurrying to the window and securing it firmly. "I'm sorry, I thought Mavis had closed the windows up for the evening." She cast a cursory glance towards the clock on the mantel. "I hope nothing keeps you up at this late hour, sir? Can I fetch you anything? Perhaps a warm drink?"

"No," Darcy said, more sharply than he intended. He followed the word with a polite grimace in lieu of a smile, and his housekeeper ducked into a half curtsey, before excusing herself.

The room felt even emptier, somehow, in her absence, and with reluctance, Darcy turned towards bed, acknowledging to himself that it was late in the evening and he'd serve nobody well by forcing himself into wakefulness simply out of some obstinate desire to rule over his need for sleep. It was on this final retreat towards the door when he ensured the fire was out, and snatched up a remaining candle to light his way upstairs, that he noticed another casualty of the cold night air's onslaught. A pile of papers had been whisked off his desk and onto the floor, and with a grunt, he stooped to retrieve them. He dropped the pile back onto the mahogany desk, vowing he would sort through them on the morrow, when a certain word caught his eye and made him pause. It was his own hand and spelt out the very names that had been on the tip of his tongue half the evening. *Bennet...Longbourn...Netherfield.* He scanned the missive, unable to place it for a moment, before recognising it as a letter he had only half-finished addressing to Georgiana. His account of life at Meryton had been interrupted by the sudden decision to uproot and abandon Hertfordshire in favour of London, and he had gone no further with the letter.

Yet even now it haunts me! he thought, ruefully sliding the piece of paper free and folding it neatly. He carried it with him to bed, intending on reading it over once more before disposing of it. Georgiana would have a fresh letter, one without mention of the Bennet sisters, although he was sure she would wish for more intelligence concerning their near neighbours, for he had mentioned them in passing in his previous note, and received, in her reply, a demand for more detail. *Gentlemen never feel the necessity of description,* she had complained. *How am I to imagine the people of whom you write if you cannot even spare a line or two to tell me of their looks? This Miss Bennet that Mr Bingley is already attached to - for I assume that to be the case, though you said nothing so clearly in your letter and I have resorted to looking for all that you did not express - must be very beautiful, but what is the nature of her appearance? Is she fair-haired or dark? Short or tall? Dainty or plump? And her sisters, are they all very different creatures, or all in a mode one after another? Tell me more, William, for I am lonely and eager for some distraction from my own consuming thoughts at present. Better yet -* and these words had made him smile when he read them. *Invite me to stay. Mr Bingley will not mind, and his sister, I am sure, is as sweet-natured as he and would welcome another guest at Netherfield. Merely send word and I can be with you before Christmas!* He had not sent word, of course, nor would he, for Georgiana would be overwhelmed by the busyness of London, particularly London at Christmas.

Tucking the note into his pocket he reached his room and continued to ready himself for bed, grateful that the memory of his sister had turned his thoughts from freely rampaging about the countryside back to something approaching order. It was not befitting to allow them to roam so, and it was pointless to dwell on people he had left so firmly behind him. So he had seen a lady who, in passing, bore a vague resemblance to Elizabeth Bennet. Did that mean he must forevermore be haunted by her bright eyes and teasing tone of voice, even here and in his own home?

"It is a nonsense," he told his reflection, taking one last cursory glance in the mirror before extinguishing the candle and finding his way towards the bed in the dark. He pulled his blankets to his chin and stared up into the blackness. "She is nothing to me. Hertfordshire is nothing to me. I was there at Bingley's request only."

His whisper brought him almost entirely back to his senses, and he felt his eyelids grow heavy.

He had been in Hertfordshire at Bingley's request, and now he was in London at Bingley's request. Perhaps he ought to start eschewing his friends and decide on his own course of action if such removals were to leave him thus unsettled.

A bird screeched somewhere in the blackness of London, the last sound Darcy heard, as he surrendered to sleep...

Chapter Two

"Kitty, stop that!"

"Mama! This is so unfair! Make her stop!"

"Girls, have you no compassion on my nerves? And where is your sister? Elizabeth? *Elizabeth!*"

Lizzy had successfully managed to find a moment of sanctuary hiding in the window seat behind the drapes, ignoring the chaos that surrounded her by sheer force of will. Her concentration was fixed on her book with such intensity that the fingers that clasped tight hold of it turned white with effort. She had read the page before her twice, she knew, yet she could not recall a single word of its contents, so distracted was she by the bickering of her sisters. *And Mama*, she thought, with a glower that could rival that usually seen upon the countenance of a certain gentleman who had absented himself quite abruptly from Hertfordshire, and whom she had no cause to miss. *Why then must he plague me by invading my memories at every opportunity?* she thought, grimly pulling the curtain aside to reveal her hiding place.

"What is it, Mama?" she asked, setting her book aside and hopping down from the windowsill to be of whatever assistance Mrs Bennet required this time.

"Oh! Lizzy! There you are." Mrs Bennet sighed.

"Were you hiding in there this whole time?" Lydia asked, incredulous.

"What on earth for?" Kitty echoed, peering over Elizabeth's shoulder. "It does not look at all comfortable a seat...."

"She was spying!" Lydia said, triumphantly.

"Well, I do think that an unkind trick -"

"GIRLS!" Mrs Bennet sank into a chair, beckoning Elizabeth closer with a plump arm. "Lizzy, where is Jane? I hoped she might be with you, walking somewhere."

"It is raining, Mama," Elizabeth said, patiently. "And you know Jane has not been at all well these past few days." She bit her lip. "In fact, this morning she seems worse. I really do think we might consider sending for a doctor."

"A doctor?" Mrs Bennet's eyes flew open. "And how, pray, would we pay for him?"

"Mama, Jane is very unwell -"

"Jane is tired, and perhaps a little lovesick -"

This provoked a smothered giggle from her two sisters that Elizabeth successfully silenced with one sharp look.

"And what if she is? She has borne a dreadful disappointment." Lizzy folded her arms stiffly across her front. "I still think you were wrong to encourage her in such an attachment when this was always likely to be the case."

"How could I have known Mr Bingley would be so cruel as to abandon poor Jane? I was certain he felt an affection for her..." Mrs Bennet hesitated, appearing on the brink of tears herself. While Jane's tears were a jar to Elizabeth's own heart, her mother's were not to be borne for entirely different reasons.

"Mama -"

"I only wish for my daughters to be happily and successfully married, is that such a bad thing?" Mrs Bennet let out a wail, and Lizzy turned away, hoping to hide the irritation that flickered across her face.

"Oh, I see you turn away from me, Elizabeth, as if you despair of my feelings, which are so deep, so genuine -"

Mrs Bennet's words descended into an indecipherable sniffle, and Elizabeth took a step nearer, laying what she hoped was a conciliatory hand on her mother's shoulder.

"You must not cry, Mama," she said. "Truly, Mr Bingley is the least of our concerns. Jane's health worries me greatly, though, and I do hope you will consider sending for a doctor."

"I will consider it," Mrs Bennet said, her words muffled by her handkerchief. "But are you sure it is so very bad? It is nought but a cold, surely?"

It was a cold when she was bound to stay at Netherfield, Lizzy thought. *Now it seems far worse.* She had been sure her sister had fully recovered from the bought of ill-health that Mrs Bennet had accidentally engineered, which calamity served to secure Mr Bingley's heart, to begin with. But with the Netherfield party's departure for the capital, Jane had sunk once more into herself, first despairing at the loss of Mr Bingley who, Lizzy now had reason to believe, she truly cared for in spite of their mother's interference. She had taken Jane's silence for low spirits, but that had evolved into a bought of sickness so severe that her happy sister had kept almost entirely to her bed for two days straight complaining of a headache, and with breathing so heavy and ragged that Lizzy grew increasingly concerned.

"I do hope we shall not all be ill in time for Christmas," Lydia remarked, with a sniff.

"How does it start, do you think?" Kitty asked, her eyes wide. "For I have had a stomach ache all day."

"You have a stomach ache because you ate too much at breakfast, nothing more," Lydia said, dismissively. "But my head begins to ache." She lifted a hand in an affectation of suffering that had clearly been practised before the looking-glass, and it was all Elizabeth could do to refrain from rolling her eyes.

"I am sure it is nothing too serious," she said, determined to appear calm. Confessing her true concerns had not had the result she had wished: that her family might take Jane's condition seriously and seek to help, rather than turn their care upon themselves, as was their habit. "I will go and sit with her awhile, if you do not need me here, Mama," she said, preparing to mount her escape.

"Very well," Mrs Bennet said. "Tell me, where is Mary?"

"I believe she is in Meryton with Mr Collins," Elizabeth said, recalling seeing the pair set off at a pace that morning. "The rain will no doubt keep them there a little longer."

"Good." Mrs Bennet's words were muttered, but Elizabeth could not help but agree with the sentiment. Since Mary had accepted Mr Collins proposal - his third in as many weeks, this time met with rather more pleasure than those he offered Jane and Lizzy - she had become increasingly insufferable. Why they would not marry and depart for Hunsford, Lizzy could not tell, except that Mary was rather enjoying her position as self-appointed saviour of the Bennets. She had taken to remarking, "when I am mistress of Longbourn," as if it were a position she quite looked forward to - never pausing to realise that in so doing she was hastening the demise of her father. Mr Bennet did not miss the joke, although the more often his middle daughter spoke of life after his passing, the less amusing he found it, and he had taken to excusing himself as soon as she opened her mouth to utter the perpetual refrain.

"We might have gone with them," Kitty lamented. "At least then there might be something to do."

"Yes," Lydia exclaimed, irritably. "Visiting the poor and the sick. What need we to be in Meryton for that, when our own sister is kind enough to grace us with it in our own home." She laughed, evidently finding herself quite the wittiest young woman in a mile radius. "In any case, we would be trapped there now, forced to listen to Mr Collins sermonize all afternoon until a break in the weather might permit us to return." She shook her head vehemently. "No thank you. I am content to remain at home all day if he is gone and Mary with him."

"Then might you remain a little more quietly?" Lizzy asked, reaching the doorway. "I am hopeful Jane has managed to sleep and is thus feeling a little more herself - but if you insist on making noise that won't happen."

Kitty opened her mouth to protest, but one look from Elizabeth silenced her, and instead, she slumped into a chair with a huff, pulling Lydia down with her. They glanced around for some entertainment, at last seizing upon their workbasket, and picking at it lethargically and without enthusiasm. Still, it would suffice in keeping them still and relatively quiet for a quarter hour or more. Elizabeth pulled the door closed quietly behind her and was about to ascend the stairs when her father's voice reached her.

"Lizzy?"

Mr Bennet was closeted away in his study, so his voice was faint, muffled by the oak door that separated them. Tentatively, she pushed the door open.

"Is anything the matter, Father?" she asked, glancing around the door frame and smiling at Mr Bennet, who sat in his usual seat behind his desk, surrounded by papers.

"How does Jane fare?"

"I am about to go and check on her."

"Good girl." He glanced back towards his stack of papers, and Lizzy took a step closer. Her father's expression was not his usual implacable calm, and his forehead was creased in something that could only be described as anxiety.

"Is - is that all you wished to speak to me about?"

"Yes, yes," Mr Bennet said, with a smile that was not at all convincing. "And to thank you for bringing some peace to the sitting room." He smiled, then, the merest hint of humour. "The noise, you know."

"Indeed." Elizabeth smiled, darting over and dropping a spontaneous kiss on her father's weathered cheek. He seemed older to her, then, than he ever had before and she felt a sudden burst of affection for him. It was a trying time, she knew, and for all his apparent disinterest in his daughters' futures, she knew that even he had been surprised by Mr Bingley's sudden disappearance, and felt keenly the disappointment that had brought Jane so low.

It is Mr Darcy's fault, I do not doubt, Lizzy thought, with a dark frown, as she took the stairs two at a time. He had made his opinion of the Bennets plain the very first time they had met, and at last had had influence enough on his friend that he had separated two people who had been poised, Lizzy knew, to reach an agreement. *If Jane does not rally,* she thought, ignoring and acknowledging the thought at the same time. *I shall place the blame firmly upon his shoulders.*

"I'M REALLY VERY MUCH better," Jane said, with a wan smile.

"I might even believe that," Lizzy said, leaning forward and pressing a damp cloth to Jane's brow. "If you could utter the whole sentence without coughing."

"I did not say I was *completely* well," Jane acknowledged. "But compared to how I felt even two hours ago, there is much improvement." She reached for her sister's hand. "And all the more, for your company. Tell me, what on earth did you say to get Kitty and Lydia to stop squabbling?"

"I hardly know." Lizzy shook her head. "I think they tired themselves out. But as I left them bent over embroidery, I do not doubt another war will break out by the time I return."

Returning the cloth to its bowl, she moved back a little, straightening Jane's bedsheets, moving things so that they were easier to reach.

"Now, what would you like us to do?" she asked. "I could read a little if you wish, or we could talk -"

Another fit of coughing interrupted her.

"Or I could talk and you could listen."

Jane nodded, and Elizabeth made herself comfortable leaning on the pillows beside her.

"Did I tell you that I bumped into Mr Wickham yesterday on my walk to Meryton?"

Jane's eyes sparked with interest, which Elizabeth took as a silent encouragement to continue. "You know, he is a very interesting person. We walked part of the way together and had such a lively conversation that I wager him altogether more intelligent than I had been led to believe."

"On Lydia's authority," Jane put in.

"On Lydia's authority, quite right. She is not one for whom intelligence would ever rank as a particularly important trait. So I am pleased to acknowledge he has it and is quite able to converse warmly on any number of subjects."

"Such as?"

There had been a moment of silence before Jane's prompt, and Lizzy thought the interest in her sister's eyes not entirely as innocent as she made out.

"We discussed friends in common. He was pleased to hear of Mary and Mr Collins' engagement."

"Was he?"

Lizzy reddened. How was it possible that, despite sickness, her sister was still well able to deduce her moods from the very words she uttered or did not utter? *An agreement? Well, that is very good news, Miss Elizabeth. I half-feared that you would be the one to accept his suit, however grudgingly...*

"I rather think he mirrored my own feelings back to me, for you know I am relieved that it is Mary he is pledged to marry and not either of us."

"They are well suited," Jan said, struggling to sit upright. Lizzy leaned over and re-arranged her pillows so that she might be more comfortable.

"Perhaps *too* well suited," Lizzy remarked, with a grimace, and re-told Mary's sermon of the morning, which had been encouraged with unrelenting enthusiasm by Mr Collins. *"Economy!"* she declared, mimicking his querulous voice. "Must be the watchword of Longbourn now, as it has never been in times past."

"Oh dear." Jane smiled. "And how well did Father take such censure?"

"He recalled a matter of some importance in his study and excused himself immediately from the table."

"Poor Father."

"Poor nothing." Elizabeth frowned. "He might put a stop to it so easily by reminding Mr Collins - and Mary, for she is acting as if they are married already - that he has no plan to surrender his life just at present and so they have no right to discuss his estate before his face. They act as if he already had one foot in his grave."

"He is not as young as he was," Jane mused.

"Well, that is true of all of us!" Lizzy said, scornfully. "Here we have Christmas almost upon us, and -"

"And what a quiet Christmas it shall be!" Jane sighed. "Do you recall Mr Bingley's promise of a Christmas ball? How disappointing for the others that he was called away before he could put his plan in motion."

Lizzy held her breath, surprised to hear Mr Bingley's name on Jane's lips when her sister had so far been careful to avoid it. She, too, had studiously skirted referring to Netherfield or its occupants for fear of upsetting Jane further.

"Has there - has there been any word from London?" Jane asked, with an affectation of nonchalance that fooled Lizzy not one whit.

"Silence on all fronts," she said, folding her arms across her front. "But you know how Christmas is. Things always slow down in the countryside. The opposite is true in London, I wager, so perhaps Mr Bingley finds himself too busy to write."

"Oh, I did not expect him to!" Jane said. "I only thought his sister might send a note or two. We were growing quite close, you know..."

"Hmmm." Elizabeth's response was non-committal. She did not believe Caroline Bingley capable of closeness with another person unless they served some purpose. If she feigned a friendship with Jane, it was surely with the intent of being kept aware of any closeness developing between Jane and her brother, so that she might rout it at the first available opportunity. She had certainly never hidden her true feelings for Elizabeth. In fact, Lizzy was forced to own that she almost missed the verbal sparring matches she and Caroline Bingley had engaged in, both succeeding in sliding such insults under the veil of polite conversation. It had been a challenge and an entertainment to her, particularly when faced with Mr Darcy as an alternative companion. He would sit in silence, most often, scarcely offering a word that might be considered conversation. Yet he was gone to London, too, and Longbourn felt strangely bereft without any of the Netherfield party close by.

"I am sure you miss Mr Darcy, too," Jane said, her eyes sparkling with fun.

"You must be recovering," Lizzy countered. "For you have rediscovered your sense of humour." She frowned, affecting concern. "Or are you delirious, Jane dear, that you might make such a suggestion." She reached a hand out to Jane's forehead. "Yes, feverish! That will explain your error. If there is one person in all of Hertfordshire who I do *not* miss in his absence it is Mr Fitzwilliam Darcy. London is welcome to keep him forever, it makes no difference to me!"

Chapter Three

At last, there was a break in the weather long enough to permit the consideration of a walk, and Elizabeth seized her opportunity. She did not care that the day's deluge had left the ground beneath her feet muddy in extreme, nor did she pause in her progress to think of the damage such a surface would do to her petticoats. She recalled, grimly, the last time she had walked with such energy in such conditions: the day of her flight, on foot, to Netherfield to assure herself of Jane's well-being. It had quite scandalised the Netherfield party, she felt sure of that, having been conscious of Caroline Bingley's barely whispered "*Six inches!*" Referring, she did not doubt, to the level of mud she had tracked into the house. She was sorry for any inconvenience such a bedraggled appearance might have caused her friends, but what concern could she have had for mere mud when her sister's health was in danger? Walking was the only means of transport left open to her, and so she had used it.

Today's expedition was for altogether more selfish reasons. Jane's health was no more assured, but at least she was safely resting in her own home, with her family on hand to offer support and, Lizzy hoped, sensible care. She had impressed upon Mrs Bennet and Lydia the importance of a doctor. When that had not worked, she had taken the matter to Mr Bennet, and when even he had seemed reluctant to order a doctor on account of the cost, she had decided that she, herself, would go. Not right away, and not until she was certain of the need. There was every chance Jane might rally before the day was out. *If she is no better in the morning, then I will go, and I shall bear any criticism from my family in incurring such an expense. What price can be put on my own sister's health?*

Still unbearably restless, and irritated beyond what was normal by her sisters, Lizzy had haunted the window, waiting for the first glimpse of brightness that might release her from the prison Longbourn had become. She cast a wary glance overhead. The clouds still gathered, and she felt certain this was merely a reprieve, not the end of the downpour promised for the day.

"All the more reason not to let the opportunity pass," she muttered, walking still faster, and ignoring the wet squelching of her boots in the mud. She breathed deeply, relishing the cold sting of the damp winter air, and soon began to feel better. It was amazing how a modicum of activity could work to restore peace to her tormented spirit. She was alone among her sisters in finding this, and for that, she was almost pleased, for it guaranteed she might walk without company and enjoy the peace and freedom to nurse her own thoughts as she walked.

Might Mr Bingley be contacted? Told, perhaps, of Jane's ill-health? Yet what good would such an action serve? Did Lizzy really think he might rush to Jane's bedside, and throw himself down before her, offering the declaration of love that might restore her to full health? It was a fairy-tale and not a very likely one. Lizzy frowned. Did she really wish to guilt Mr Bingley into marriage, if it meant both he and Jane would be miserable? Surely he would resent it in time, and grow to resent her sister in turn. Lizzy frowned still more fiercely. No, she would not encourage that. Jane must be loved - Jane *would* be loved - by whichever gentleman did marry her. If Mr Bingley was too stupid or weak to do so, in spite of the prejudices of his sister and friend, well, then he did not deserve her.

"Miss Elizabeth!"

It took a second call before the gentleman's voice managed to successfully break through Lizzy's thoughts, and a further moment for the interruption to fully arrest her movements. She stopped, momentarily confused, for she had been so deeply lost in her own tumultuous thoughts that she scarcely noticed where she was.

"Mr Wickham!" The figure of her friend came into view, and he jogged the few steps towards her, closing the space between them in a moment. "What brings you to this part of the county?"

"I might declare it is your own fair self. I felt compelled by some sprite to take a walk in this very direction and thus cross your path quite as if providence herself directed it!" He laughed, a bright, jolly sound that lifted Elizabeth's spirits considerably more than her walk alone had managed. "Alas that would be a falsehood, and I do not doubt you would see right through it, Miss Elizabeth, for you do not strike me as a particularly fanciful lady."

"I am not entirely sure that is a compliment!" Elizabeth admitted, with a self-deprecating smile. "Nonetheless, I will agree with your assessment. I am afraid I have a practical streak within me that deters me from too much daydreaming."

"Exactly as it should be, for you would be not half such an engaging companion if your mind was always away with the fairies." Wickham glanced over her shoulder. "And yet I believe I find you out walking alone, and surely that cannot be. Where are your sisters?"

"At home," Lizzy said, cheerfully. "Not a one of them could be pressed to accompany me. Well, Mary at least is otherwise engaged - she and Mr Collins are in Meryton. And Jane-" She trailed off, suddenly shy of speaking about Jane's deteriorating health with her new friend. "Jane is a little unwell."

"I see." Wickham's features became serious, and Lizzy detected a note of compassion that made her rue her caution. He would take her concern seriously, she knew. More seriously than her family did, at any rate. And it would be good to confide in someone the true nature of her fears for Jane, without needing always to watch her words and tend to the feelings of others less able to bear the truth than she.

"In truth, she is more than a little unwell." Lizzy sighed. "I am quite worried about her health."

"Is there anything I can do to help?" Wickham glanced back up the path. "Meryton is not far, might I go for a doctor on your behalf? Or at least accompany you on your errands. Perhaps the apothecary will have some tincture that may help. We might take a carriage back so that speed might be of chief concern."

"You are very kind, Mr Wickham," Lizzy said, touched by his suggestions. "But I have agreed to wait, at least for a little while, before proceeding to the doctor. Father is certain she will rally."

"I dare say he is correct." Wickham nodded, slowly, as if digesting this information and weighing its veracity in his own mind before speaking again. "When someone one cares about is unwell it can often seem catastrophic - more so than the same symptoms in one we did not know well. It is impossible to be impartial in such a case, and so the situation appears far more grave than it may be in actuality."

"Quite right!" Lizzy laughed. "And so, you see, I am perhaps a little more fanciful than you attest. My sister falls ill, and I am immediately convinced she is at death's door."

"Nonsense! I dare say you are right to have such a concern, and righter still to manage it. Perhaps give it another day, and if she still languishes, well, then you might be entirely justified in seeking a medical opinion." He smiled. "On the other hand, she will likely rally and all that will have been achieved by your anxiety is a proof of what a good sister you are. So really, there is no harm to be felt."

Lizzy was suitably cheered by this assessment, and her mood lifted still further when Wickham offered her his arm.

"Perhaps you might permit me to walk a little way with you, Miss Elizabeth? I think you will agree with me that walking is always more enjoyable when it is undertaken with a friend..."

"I CANNOT OWN I AM DISAPPOINTED to hear of his departure," Wickham said. He and Elizabeth had been walking but a few minutes before their conversation turned to their mutual acquaintance. Lizzy recalled what Mr Wickham had said of Mr Darcy previously, and was not surprised that her friend was happy to see the back of him.

"Yet I see he is still up to his old tricks. Fitzwilliam Darcy can no more let a man alone without interfering than he can exist an hour without passing judgment on the rest of us and finding us wanting."

Elizabeth gasped, surprised to hear such vitriol in the usually cheerful Wickham's voice. Her reaction evidently tempered his, for he stopped walking a moment, and shot her a smile that was part penitent, part rueful, and all charming.

"Ah, you do not approve of me speaking so vehemently of a man I have already confessed to disliking. I dare say you are right, Miss Elizabeth, and I ought to guard my tongue a little better. Forgive me. I cannot help but speak the truth as I see it, and hang the consequences." He hesitated, lowering his gaze momentarily. "Although, I do hope the consequences of speaking so just now are not so very dire. I would hate to think that a bad-tempered outburst might be enough to cost me your good opinion."

"As if I could be so quick to judge!" she exclaimed. "Surely you confuse me with the gentleman to whom you refer." She shook her head. "A notion to which I take the greatest objection. Mr Darcy is quick to form opinions, and even quicker to form judgments, from which he can apparently never be swayed. I would hate to be like him."

"However could you be like him? He, who always grimaces and frowns as if his mere existence is a cause of displeasure to him - or perhaps it is the existence of anyone else in the world besides himself, for I dare say he certainly spares no good feeling in that quarter. He thinks himself far superior to the rest of us mere mortals." His expression softened into a sly smile. "No, the only manner I would suggest you were alike was in your expression on my approach. Your frown was so fierce as you walked that I thought "that expression surely was learned from Mr Darcy. Poor Miss Elizabeth! I do hope she might be brought out of it with all speed." Of course, when you confided the reason for your expression, I repented of the thought. If ever a person had reason to frown it would be you, out of concern for your sister. Mr Darcy can have no such excuse, and yet his expression is fierce on almost every occasion. The poor man must be close to doing himself an injury. I wonder that he does not scare himself, whenever he should happen to catch a glimpse of his scowl in a mirror."

Elizabeth laughed, then stopped, suddenly. The teasing tone in Mr Wickham's voice had become altogether unkind, bordering on cruel, and she thought his comments unnecessarily mean, even to one as doubtlessly deserving as Mr Darcy.

"He cannot help it, I suppose. And I must own that he does not always frown. I have seen him smile."

"You never have!" Mr Wickham laughed. "Well, wonders will never cease. How came you to witness such a feat?"

"We were pressed into dancing together - a circumstance I wager he found as disagreeable as I did, for he is not fond of dancing, I believe."

"And yet your company was so delightful that it provoked a smile in spite of his unhappy occupation?"

"I very much doubt that! Indeed, I confess to being rather unkind to poor Mr Darcy."

"*Poor* Mr Darcy? Is he to be pitied now?"

"I think anyone who cannot find amusement in life, enough goodness to make one smile in spite of the little suffering each one of us is afflicted with, ought to be pitied. But you distract me from my story." She shook her head, warningly, at her companion, and continued. "We were dancing together and I tried my best to engage *poor Mr Darcy -*" here she paused, and Wickham nodded, contritely, encouraging her to continue uninterrupted. "In conversation. We attempted two or three topics, I scarcely recall them now, with little success, for as I said, neither one of us were particularly happy to be forced together. Yet at last he turned to books - I rather think by this point he was grasping at straws. He knew me to be fond of reading, and I do not doubt he wished mercy to prompt me into a monologue that he might no longer be impressed upon to talk, merely listen to me hold forth. Of course, I refused, and instead challenged him to name one book we might both have encountered and thus be free to discuss together."

"Of course he failed?"

"He did not try! I am sorry to say that very soon after that the dance ended and we parted ways. And that is the last time our paths crossed."

"I spy a problem in your story, Miss Eliza," Wickham said, that lazy smile drawing upon his features once more. "You promised me evidence that Mr Darcy wore a smile."

"It was upon first mentioning books - and I confess it did a great deal to improve his countenance. What a pity he might not wear a smile more often, then we might be able to tolerate him a little better."

"And here I feel certain it is not Miss Elizabeth Bennet I am talking with at all, but her young sister. For it is Miss Lydia whose chief concern is beauty: I felt certain her sister rather more swayed by what is contained within a fellow's head than the appearance of his features. Tell me the truth - you walk with me only because I am tolerably handsome and not because you find any value whatsoever in my conversation. Admit it! Your true nature is revealed."

"Mr Wickham!" Elizabeth could not help but laugh out loud at the pantomime being performed before her. "You are nonsensical!"

"And yet I notice you do not refute my claim." He grinned, a sly, amused smile, that Elizabeth found herself returning. Their eyes met and she found herself at that moment unable to look away. His comments had been made in jest, yet in one aspect Elizabeth found him to be utterly truthful: he was indeed handsome, with an easy smile and blue eyes which were as disingenuous as Mr Darcy's dark ones were stormy. *Of course, I care little enough for appearances...* This was true too: if all Wickham had to recommend him were his looks she certainly would not find his company so appealing. But he was clever, too, and witty. Why, they had been walking together almost a mile and she had scarcely noticed the passing of time.

There was a crack of thunder overhead, and a fat raindrop landed with decision upon her head, followed by another, then another.

"Oh!" she cried.

"Here, let us shelter beneath that tree." Mr Wickham did not permit her any time to debate, for he grabbed her hand and fairly pulled her along behind him, reaching the shelter of the evergreen boughs just in time, for the rain began again with a vengeance. They were offered a little shelter, provided they stayed close to the trunk of the great tree, and it was then that Elizabeth realised that her fingers were still entwined with Mr Wickham's, and she slipped her hand free, blushing a little at the closeness of contact, and circling both her arms around herself, partly because of the sudden drop in temperature that accompanied the downpour but partly, she acknowledged, by way of self-protection. The precariousness of her position suddenly dawned on her. Here she was out walking, alone, with a gentleman she knew barely anything of.

Untrue, she countered her conscience, jutting her chin out in a silent act of defiance. *I know him to be amiable, and a gentleman. He is a member of the regiment, after all. What more do I need to know?*

"I hope you will not get into trouble upon your return," Wickham remarked, lightly, as he looked out across the fields that were now rendered hazy by rain that fell in rods. "I know it is not entirely respectable, being caught out in a rainstorm with a gentleman with whom you have no - agreement." His voice changed, slightly, on this last word, and Elizabeth's ears caught the drop in tone. At length, he looked back towards her, and she found herself once more caught by those striking blue eyes.

"I know it is not the most conventional approach, Miss Elizabeth, but you must know, that is, you must surely have gleaned some sense of my feelings for you."

Elizabeth's breath caught in her throat.

"Forgive me." Wickham took her surprise for disapproval, and took a step backwards, dropping his arms to his sides.

"No -" Elizabeth said, stumbling a step towards him, and closing the gap his movement had created. "Please, you caught me off-guard."

"Then I have misread your own affections?" There was a trace of wistfulness in his voice. "Either way, the fault is mine. I hesitated to speak any sooner, Miss Elizabeth, on account of my position, and because I thought - I wondered if perhaps you might care for another."

"Another?" An image of Mr Darcy floated before Elizabeth's eyes, and she batted it away. "Mr Wickham, believe me when I tell you that I care for no-one - that I have no existing connection with any gentleman."

"Then I might risk speaking, for it is a risk. Miss Elizabeth, I wonder, that is, I hope -"

"Lizzy!"

Wickham's words were interrupted by a high-pitched cry, and Elizabeth glanced over her shoulder in time to see a tiny figure racing towards them.

"Kitty?" She could barely make sense of the image of her younger sister hurrying towards them, ignorant of the rain and with more energy than she had exhibited all day.

"Oh, Lizzy!" Kitty sobbed, reaching their tree, and throwing her arms around her sister. She scarcely seemed to notice Mr Wickham, and certainly did not acknowledge him. "Mama bid me come to find you. They sent a servant out for the doctor. Lizzy! Jane is worse! She is much, much worse. You must come home right away!"

Elizabeth's heart plummeted, and the rain drove down harder as if nature itself reflected her impending dread.

Chapter Four

Darcy bolted upright in his bed, the thundering of the rain from Meryton mirrored in the trundle of a carriage driving past outside his house. *Strange,* he thought. *The wind must be blowing in just such a way that the sound reaches me...*

He shivered, pulling his bedsheets to his shoulders, and glanced around the room. It was his own room: in his own house, in London. And yet, just a moment before he had been sheltering under a tree, he had been with Elizabeth, and with Wickham. And yet, not there, not exactly. It was as if some spirit was tormenting him, playing out some scene from a nightmare designed to plague him. Jane Bennet gravely ill, mourning a separation he himself had orchestrated. Elizabeth deceived by Wickham. The two of them talking together, laughing, mocking him – united, in fact, by their shared dislike of him. He shuddered, but this time it was nothing to do with the temperature.

"Twas a dream," he murmured aloud. "Nought but a dream." Elizabeth Bennet had appeared in his nightly imaginings merely because he had been thinking of her so shortly before turning in to bed. And why had he been thinking of her? Because she seemed set to haunt his daily as well as nightly imaginings. *It is she herself haunting me, all the way from Hert-*

fordshire. His lip curled in an amused half-smile. He was no lover of the gothic, and yet today he seemed to have slipped between the pages of just such a novel as those he despaired of Georgiana reading. He was Udolpho, plagued by mystery. Or Faust, with his past failings paraded before him. He shook his head. "Certainly, whatever I am, I am in need of sleep and good sense." How long had it been since a dream so disturbed him? And a dream that was full of the normal everyday life of a family in Hertfordshire he hardly cared for. It was imagining, only, and yet what if it wasn't? His heart constricted at the thought that this was not mere fiction, but a version of what was daily occurring behind him in Hertfordshire. He blinked, willing the memories to fade. What mattered it to him who Elizabeth Bennet chose to associate with? That she might be deceived by Wickham: that was the cause of his dismay. He certainly cared little enough who she formed attachments with. It was not as if he, Darcy, had ever intended on making her an offer.

He raked a hand through his dark hair and was relieved to feel his breathing return to normal. His pounding heart receded, and the dream itself began to fade from his memory. It was not so very unusual, he reasoned, to find one's thoughts returning to a place one left behind as recently has he had quit Hertfordshire. Nor was it so very strange to see the Bennets as a key feature of his dreams, as they had been the reason behind his sudden removal to London, intentionally or otherwise. That it was Elizabeth in particular to whom his thoughts returned was also perhaps of little enough significance. He could admit, here, in a darkened room with only his own self to acknowledge the truth, that his first assessment of Elizabeth Bennet had been wrong. Formed hastily, and in an attempt to deflect Charles Bingley's well-intentioned enquiry, he had dismissed Elizabeth as beneath his notice. How could she be, however, when he found her to be lively, spirited, intelligent and interesting, quite the most fascinating creature who had ever before crossed his path? And to think her placed in the middle of so unsuitable a family, in so unprepossessing a place as Longbourn? He shook his head in wonder. It was a nonsense, pure and simple. An impossible nonsense and he would do well to remove all thought of it from his mind.

He turned his pillow over so that he might find the cool side when again he lay down, staring into the blackness and waiting for sleep to find him.

I will not return to Longbourn, he instructed his subconscious. *I will not return to Elizabeth Bennet, or to Wickham, or to Longbourn. I will not...*

Chapter Five

St James' Park was crowded at the best of times. At Christmas, when half of England who was not usually predisposed to be in London found itself there, it became unbearable.

"Oh, good morning, Mrs Rackham." Making a show of greeting any acquaintance she thought worthy of acknowledgement, Caroline Bingley's voice took on an obsequious, snivelling tone that grated on Darcy's nerves and merely increased his discomfort.

How came I to agree to this, anyway? he thought, walking with a polite two feet of distance between himself and Caroline. Charles was nowhere to be seen, and every few steps Caroline would shift a fraction closer to him. In answer, he would alter his course to restore the distance, as such that in a few short minutes he was almost scraping his boots on the grass at the edge of the path. He stopped, nodding a greeting towards some acquaintance, and determined that he would ask Caroline directly what her plans were for the evening. He was not entirely oblivious to her contentment with their current progress around the park. They walked with slow enough pace that they could not be mistaken for a pair of strangers - yet with the distance Darcy maintained in the hope that they would not be assumed to be courting, no matter what Caroline's hopes were on that subject. They were walking slow enough, however, to be forced to stop and greet those who passed them that they recognised which, it seemed to Darcy, was practically everyone.

Is all of London in St. James' Park this afternoon?

There. It was afternoon. Why could he not remember what pre-empted their visit to the park? Surely there must have been some chance, some slight opportunity he had clearly missed when he might have refused the suggestion of a walk. Why, then, had he not taken it? And where, in heavens' name, was Charles?

"Oh, look, Mr Darcy!" Caroline trilled, raising her hand in a languid wave. "There is Charles and Miss Parker. Why, we must have walked a quite a pace, for I believe we have completed an entire circuit of the park in the time it has taken them to move but a few yards." Her eyes sparkled. "But perhaps they have been too busy in conversation to focus very intently on exercise."

"Perhaps," Darcy said, drily. He was pleased to see Charles, hoping that his friend might prove a worthy buffer in between him and Caroline, yet the presence of another lady on Charles' arm would lend their party an altogether romantic air he did not entirely rejoice in. Perhaps he would attempt to engage this young lady in conversation and leave Charles to his sister for a few moments. He frowned. The notion of engaging another young lady - a stranger to him, and one so richly attired and sociable as the *Miss Parker* on Charles' arm appeared to be - there, she stopped to speak to yet another couple that passed, and not merely a "good afternoon" as Darcy so often insisted upon. She was stopping to speak for several moments and with great animation. Darcy shuddered. The appeal of trading the familiar, if tiresome, Caroline Bingley for this new young lady plummeted with his heart into his boots.

"Good afternoon, Charles," he said, as they drew level with the couple. He nodded, curtly, to Miss Parker, certain they must have been at least introduced, for their party seemed to have arrived at the park together, and separated quite naturally, although Darcy possessed no memory of either event, and felt quite certain he had never laid eyes on Miss Parker before in his life. *I have met others like her, though,* he acknowledged, thinking fleetingly that she was a poor comparison to Jane Bennet. He blinked. Where on earth had such a thought come from? Had the very intention of bringing Charles to London not been to separate him from Miss Bennet? Surely if Charles formed an attachment to another that could only aid in the breaking of that first, foolish match.

Yet even as he thought this, he recognised its inaccuracy. Was Charles really so foolish to forfeit affection with Miss Jane Bennet? She was pretty - prettier even than this new Miss Parker, and in an altogether more pleasing manner, it seemed to Darcy. Miss Parker's features were rather too strong for her face and rendered still more so by the sheer quantity of jewels that sparkled about her. Her clothing was too bright, almost garish. Better suited to a ballroom than a walk, and he wagered, from the pinched nature of her smile, that her shoes were not designed for walking.

"Caroline!" Miss Parker tottered over, throwing her arms around Caroline Bingley as if the two were long-lost sisters. Caroline, he noticed, with a smirk, did not return the gesture with half so much enthusiasm as that with which it was offered. "Isn't it a beautiful afternoon?"

"Beautiful." Caroline's response was wooden and offered as if through clenched teeth. Darcy noticed she did not meet her friend's smile, but that her eyes were fixed on Charles, who stood limply to one side, watching the interaction yet scarcely appearing to notice it at all.

"You were so kind to invite me, and Mr Bingley and I have been having a fascinating conversation," Miss Parker continued, blushing at the words "Mr Bingley" as if she could control the reaction almost entirely. Darcy frowned, wondering if this performance was fooling Caroline. It certainly seemed to be having little enough effect on Charles or, indeed, on him. Miss Annabelle Parker was, it seemed to Darcy, the very kind of woman he had first imagined Jane Bennet to be. She was determined upon snaring Charles Bingley for her husband and was bald in her attempts to win his heart. It was straight out of the manipulative young lady's handbook, of which Darcy was certain Caroline had a copy. Had she not tried almost this very approach with him? First, flattering one's conversation as witty, or intelligent, or fascinating. It did not really matter which. Secondly, dropping the name of every fashionable or respectable person one had ever come into contact with, even claiming them as friends who one had scarcely passed one quarter-hour's conversation with. Miss Parker was helped here, of course, by virtue of their being in St. James' park and faced with a passing parade of the elegant and respectable upon whom one might hang such a narrative. Next would surely be an invitation to call.

As if his thoughts had been spoken aloud, Miss Parker cleared her throat.

"Dear me, it is so very cold this afternoon!" She shivered, with great effect, and eyeballed Charles. He hardly noticed. "Do not you think, Mr Bingley?" Miss Parker tried again, but Charles studiously avoided being brought into the conversation. "I said, I do think it so very cold -"

"Yes," Caroline snapped, then smiled, attempting to wrangle control of her temper once more. "Yes, Annabelle dear, it is very cold. Why don't we find somewhere we might shelter for a while?"

"Oh! Well, my dear, I was just going to say, why not return to my house, for it is quite close by."

Caroline's eyes narrowed, and Darcy fancied he could read her thoughts.

Close by? I very much doubt it.

"I know of an inn but two minutes' walk from the park," he offered, wanting for reasons he could not quite articulate to relocate somewhere out of the glare of the entirety of London, and thinking that if he could not shake off the attentions of Caroline Bigley and Annabelle Parker, at least he might not be forced to endure them without refreshment.

"What say you, Charles? The Stag. It is pleasant enough for the ladies, don't you agree?"

"Eh?" Charles glanced up all of a sudden as if called back from obliviousness by Darcy's question. He frowned. "Sorry, what did you say?"

"The Stag, Charles." Caroline tossed her head. "Mr Darcy is suggesting we might move to an inn and take some refreshments." She turned to Darcy and smiled, a strange, knowing smile, that commanded a response, but he was not sure of what nature. Instead, he willed his features to remain impassive, neither rewarding nor punishing Caroline for her acquiescence.

A FEW SHORT MOMENTS later, the party was contentedly nestled around a small table in one corner of the inn, which was pleasantly busy, and not populated by anyone that either lady might seek to impress. These were good men, gentlemen and barristers, the sort that Darcy might not lament being forced to converse with. They none of them cared for matters of marriage or society gossip and it was for that reason that Darcy had suggested it as a destination, being aware of several tea shops just as close to the park where their small party would have garnered more than a passing interest from the gossips and maiden aunts who frequented such places.

The ladies fell to discussing their hats, and thence the critical assessment of the fashions adopted by their compatriots that afternoon. Once he could be certain that their attention was fully engrossed in one another, he leaned closer to Bingley and spoke, in a low voice.

"It is good to see you taking some exercise. What a shame there is no shooting to be had, eh?"

This topic was specifically designed to attract Bingley's attention, for Darcy recalled more than one occasion when the two gentlemen had gone shooting and his friend had proved enthusiastic, if not well-skilled.

"Yes." Charles raised his glass to his lips. "Tis a pity. But I dare say it is for the best." He darted a glance towards his sister as if waiting for her to contradict him.

The two gentlemen fell into silence once more.

"Miss Parker seems a...pleasant creature." Darcy voiced this carefully, determined to show no partiality in either way towards the mention of Miss Parker.

"Is she?" Charles frowned. "I mean, yes, yes. Amiable. Pleasant. Very much." He sighed.

Darcy raised his eyebrows. Charles must be suffering indeed if he was so difficult to goad into conversation. Generally, in his experience, Charles was harder to quiet than he was to encourage in speaking.

"Has Miss Bingley heard any news from Hertfordshire?" he asked, at last, wondering why he felt a sudden compulsion to mention the family both he and Caroline had up until now intended to ignore. "From Miss Bennet, perhaps?"

"Miss Bennet?" Charles darted a wounded glance towards Darcy. "No, there has been no word, at least, none that Caroline has shared with me. Have you - have you heard anything?"

There was a note of desperation in Charles' voice that quelled Darcy's desire to laugh at the suggestion that he, of any of them, might have received letters from Longbourn. He shook his head.

"Mind you, it is Christmas." He might have been an accomplice to Caroline Bingley in separating Charles from Jane Bennet, but he could not so easily tolerate seeing his friend so bereft. He began to wonder if he had been too harsh, too hasty. Just because certain women - and he included the engaging Miss Parker in this assessment - sought to secure Charles Bingley in an effort to secure his fortune and their own future, he wondered, not for the first time, if Jaen Bennet could really be included among their number. Had it perhaps been a throwaway comment that had steered him in this direction, pitted him against her? Certainly, her sister did not share the intent of marrying for wealth and position, or she might have acted rather more warmly towards him, seeking to overcome any disagreement, rather than being pitched to continue it. A wry smile crept onto his features. No, Miss Elizabeth Bennet did not intend to make herself agreeable to any gentleman of wealth in order to secure marriage. Her other sisters, too, seemed hardly to care what others thought of them, if their behaviour at Meryton was anything to go by. He had been horrified by their common flirting and laughter, but now he was forced to admit they were at least the actions of honest young ladies. Who knew but that Miss Parker was predisposed to just the same activity, only she had kept it firmly under control whilst in the presence of her potential beau? He blinked, startled to see his thoughts taking such a turn. Since when did he approve of young women making a spectacle of themselves over polite comportment befitting their position? And since when was honesty more important than appearance? *Must one choose between the two characteristics?* he thought, with a sigh.

"Dear me!" Caroline's voice broke through his confused thoughts. "Between you and my brother, Mr Darcy, we are half a very sorry table indeed." She laughed, but it was not quite so musical as she evidently intended it to be. Darcy shifted in his seat and managed to summon up a polite smile.

"Charles," Caroline barked. "I do not think you have heard a word dear Annabelle has said this past ten minutes! Do not disappoint poor Miss Parker, for I have assured her you are a most avid conversationalist."

Suitably chastened, Charles straightened in his chair, and turned his attention, reluctantly, towards Annabelle Parker.

His features became serene, once more, but Darcy noticed they lacked the animation they had possessed whenever Charles was pressed into society with Jane Bennet. What he had considered merely a passing flirtation was clearly far more, at least as far as Charles was concerned. With Darcy's mounting doubts over his hasty assessment of Miss Bennet, he wondered if he and Caroline had acted wisely in removing Charles so immediately and completely from their circle.

He turned to Caroline to ask if she, too, had received no word from Hertfordshire, surprised to find the suggestion that she, herself, write was on the tip of his tongue. She spoke before him, however, and silenced any suggestion he might make.

"Mr Darcy, I do hope you plan to attend the Parkers' ball tomorrow night. It should be a most enjoyable occasion."

"I do not believe I have had the pleasure of an invitation." Darcy was not too disappointed to have been thus overlooked. His response caught at Annabelle Parker's ear, though, and she turned, with a too-wide smile, towards him.

"Oh, indeed! Mr Darcy, you must come!" Her eyes slid momentarily towards Caroline and then back to his. "I was sure you were invited, for my parents are eager to see you again."

Eager to see me again? Darcy swallowed a groan. He had spoken but four words to Mr Samuel Parker in all their association, and less than that to his wife. But he knew they were fond of exploiting what connections they had, and no doubt intended on including him towards that end. Their whole London set would likely be there, and so he must go or face being discussed at length in his absence.

"In that case, I will gladly attend." Darcy's words belied their truth. *Gladly*, no. But attend, he would, if only to offer Charles some solace from the so-far, so-unsubtle matchmaking being played out before him by that gentleman's sister and the very lady whose home would host their gathering.

Caroline's smile could only be described as radiant, as if Darcy had paid her the highest of compliments in acquiescing to the invitation of her friends. Too late, Darcy felt a sense of foreboding steal over him. He had played unwittingly into their trap, he was certain of that now, yet what the end result would be remained a mystery.

It will all be revealed tomorrow night, I expect, he thought, attending to his meal with grim satisfaction. *And no doubt I will rue my attention to convention. Another ball, another party. How I loathe London at Christmas time!*

Chapter Six

Almost immediately, the ball was upon them, and Darcy felt certain he had but blinked and been transported from the inn to the front steps of the Parkers' townhouse, which was ostentatious in its appearance, far outstripping his own modest abode. There was something lacking in the taste applied to the house's design, however, so that it stood out from its companions for all the wrong reasons. The adornments were too much, too striking, and it gave the house an almost comical appearance, that had not been helped by the great swathes of additional decorations that had been applied to it in celebration of the festive season. Darcy swallowed his groan as he approached the front door, but could barely succeed in mustering a grimace, let alone a smile.

"Mr Darcy! Jolly good to see you again. And how do we find you this evening?"

"You find me as content as ever I could be." He bowed, already irritated by Mr Parker's too-warm welcome. "And you, sir? How is your family?"

"Well, well!" Mr Parker grasped him in a hearty handshake such that Darcy struggled to free himself from straight away, and was instead wheeled around and paraded in front of at least half a dozen of Mr Parker's other guests, none of whom he particularly wished to speak to.

"Come in, come in. My Annabelle is wild to see you!"

Indeed, Darcy thought, mentally readying himself for the spectacle of a *wild* Annabelle Parker. Fortunately, this description had been all artistry by her father, and he spotted her arm in arm with Charles Bingley, already monopolising him with every ounce of her abilities. Darcy was poised to rescue his friend, when he noticed Caroline Bingley standing on Charles' other side, surreptitiously scanning the crowd. She must be watching for his own arrival. He hesitated but a moment, wondering if it would be possible to speak to Charles without attracting the notice of his sister, but had scarcely had time to formulate a plan before Caroline called out to him, waving enthusiastically. There would be no escape for Darcy that evening, and he sighed, forcing his grimace into something approaching a smile, and went to join his friends.

"Miss Parker, Miss Bingley." He dismissed the ladies with a nod and fixed what remained of his attention on Bingley. "Charles, how do you fare this evening?"

"Well enough, Darcy." His friend actually smiled. "Though it does me good to see you here. Goodness, will you dance, as well?"

"I believe that is the occupation one must seek, at a ball," Darcy remarked, with grim acknowledgement of his evening's fate. His answer delighted the ladies, and Caroline hovered expectantly to his left. It would be a trial to dance with her, for she would take his invitation with far more weight than he intended. Yet would it be any more a trial than attempting to select a partner from a roomful of practical strangers? He glanced about him, and seeing no immediate alternative he preferred, offered his arm to Caroline. "Perhaps you would do me the honour of a dance, Miss Bingley?"

"Oh!" she trilled, her cheeks flushing with modesty he fancied was manufactured. "Oh, well, yes! Yes, Mr Darcy, I would very much like to dance with you."

He nodded, curtly, and they took their places in the crowd of other dancers, with Charles and Annabelle Parker on their other side. Darcy was pleased to see the promise of some activity lift Charles' spirits a little, although the ghost of disappointment still lurked around the edges of his friend's features.

He could not help but recall another dance that they had attended when Charles was more eager for Darcy to dance than Darcy himself was: the Meryton Assembly, the first time he had laid eyes on any one of the Bennet sisters. He had formed an immediate, and unflattering, opinion of Elizabeth Bennet, and shared it freely, though he had come to repent of it even before the evening was over. He had been so used to being surrounded by ladies such as those that occupied this particular ballroom that seeing anyone who deviated from their set pattern was unusual to him and unfortunately provoked perhaps the worst of all his personal failings: his habit of rushing to judgment. He was not often proved wrong, yet in those cases that he was the results could be dire indeed. He recalled discovering the relationship between Georgiana and George Wickham, which he had been certain was a rumour, only, passed on by a well-meaning but mistaken friend. How shaken he had been to discover the truth, but how fortunate that he had done so in time to prevent anything more serious taking place.

"You are quiet this evening, Mr Darcy," Caroline remarked, as if he was usually anything otherwise.

"Merely reserving my attention for the dancing, Miss Bingley," he responded. "I did not realise my conversation was required as well as my feet."

Caroline laughed, although his comment had not been entirely humorous. She lapsed into silence, though, taking his response for a command. He was gratified, in a way, to be left alone to his thoughts, but to some degree could not help but contrast her behaviour with Elizabeth Bennet's, who had not taken such a rebuttal to heart, and continued for the duration of their dance to attempt to engage him in conversation. It had worked poorly, but even he had been a little disappointed at how resigned they had been to silence. He had found Elizabeth interesting, although he would no more admit that to himself than he would declare it aloud to his friends.

"Oh!" Caroline exclaimed, theatrically lifting her hand to her forehead. "Oh dear! I feel dreadfully faint." She wobbled, clutching tight hold of Mr Darcy's arm, and peeled away from the crowd of dancers. "The heat!" she murmured, directing them both towards the wide windows that opened onto a dark terrace. "Oh, it is so dreadfully warm. Here, let us take a moment for some fresh air."

Darcy could no more free his arm from Caroline's vice-like grip than he could, in all good conscience, leave her, and so they both walked closer to the window, where an icy blast blew in and cooled whatever fever had caused Caroline sudden onset of dizziness.

"There, now!" she exclaimed, turning a smile that might have been called sly towards him. "Is this not a much better position to be in?"

"I rather thought you wished to dance, Miss Bingley," Darcy said, at last extricating himself from her grasp and putting a foot of space between them. "But if you are unwell, perhaps I ought to fetch your brother?"

"No!" One harsh monosyllable was softened by a short laugh. "No, do not worry Charles. I am quite well: or, rather, I will be quite well. Only do not rush away, Mr Darcy."

"Perhaps you will permit me to fetch you a chair?" he asked, seeking some occupation, anything that might give him a task to complete. This was agreed upon as being a good idea, and he turned to find a chair, moving it closer for Caroline's use. He noticed, then, the flutter of something white towards the ground, and had bent to retrieve her handkerchief, intent on returning it, before he caught sight of her expression and realised his folly.

They were quite sheltered in this particular corner, and Caroline had, he fancied, moved still closer to the terrace, where shadows might conspire to conceal them further from view. It was the last place of all that he would normally have sought to go with any young lady, for fear of their behaviour being misconstrued, wilfully or otherwise. Caroline had no such scruples, he knew, and he was certain, as the tableau played out, that this was her intent all along.

As he reached up to return her handkerchief, she moved still further away, dancing across the threshold of the ballroom to the darkened terrace.

"Miss Bingley -" he began, irritably hoping she might cease in whatever ridiculousness she was attempting before she went any further. She ignored him, and with a sigh, he stepped into the cold night air. "Your handkerchief."

"Oh, Mr Darcy!" Caroline cried, moving closer to him. "You are very kind."

Reaching to take the proffered cotton square, she caught her foot on something, real or imagined, and pitched forwards. Instinctively, Darcy reached out to break her fall and found himself pulled down with her into a pile on the floor.

He struggled to right himself quickly, glancing over to ensure they had not been seen, but he heard a couple approaching even before he managed to see them, and certainly before he managed to free himself from under Caroline's weight.

"Are you sure you do not prefer to dance, Miss Parker?" Charles asked, a little unhappily, as they approached the terrace. "I wonder - oh! Caroline! What on earth?"

AT LAST CAROLINE BINGLEY was pulled to her feet, and Darcy moved away from her quickly - but not quickly enough. He opened his mouth to justify their compromising position as an accident, nothing more, but Caroline Bingley somehow managed to speak first.

"Oh, Charles! Forgive us. We could not help ourselves, we -"

"Be quiet, Caroline." It was the sternest sentence Darcy had ever heard his friend utter and laced with the contempt that suggested he, like Darcy, grasped the true nature of what had happened. They had been found in a compromising position, certainly, but it was no more Darcy's fault than it was the accident he had been about to claim. It had been engineered - by none other than his sister.

"What's happening over there on the terrace?" A curious, middle-aged woman asked, and the two couples moved quickly back into the light.

"Nothing, Mama!" Annabelle Parker called, shooting a knowing glance at Mr Bingley. "We four were just seeking a little fresh air."

"Good, good." Mrs Parker looked a little crestfallen as if she had scented some trace of scandal in the air and was disappointed to be denied the chance of some delicious gossip.

The musicians began to play once more and the party shifted, allowing the quartet quiet enough to speak without fear of being overheard.

"Charles -" Darcy began, sensing that, of his three companions, his friend alone possessed the sense to listen to reason.

"You are a good friend to me, Darcy." Charles looked as confused as Darcy felt. "But Caroline is my sister. If anything - that is, I trust -"

"Nothing happened," Darcy said. "What could have happened? Caroline sought some fresh air and tripped. Would you rather I let her fall?"

Charles' frown darkened, and Darcy turned towards Caroline, silently willing her to corroborate his story. He knew, from one glance at her serene features, that it was a vain hope. She had done exactly as she wished, and with witnesses that would be difficult to avoid. He caught sight of a knowing look pass between the two women and his heart sank further still. He did not doubt Charles' happening to pass by the window at just such an unfortunate moment was no coincidence.

"Is that what happened?" Charles asked, directing his question to Caroline. Darcy held his breath. Everything rested on what Caroline's response would be: surely she would not lie to her brother's face?

"It is just what Mr Darcy said." Caroline's response was barely a whisper, and she dropped her eyes to the ground as if she could scarcely bear to meet her brother's gaze. Darcy felt the slightest of smiles tug at his lips and wrestled to maintain a neutral expression. *Very clever, Caroline*, he thought, realising that she had managed both to avoid lying to her brother and insinuate that Darcy's entirely truthful account was anything but accurate.

When Charles looked at him next it was with an expression that Darcy had never before seen on his friend's usually happy countenance. Reputations were at risk: his, Caroline's, but at that moment his friendship with Charles was the most precarious of all. Darcy's stomach rolled. Could he risk bringing such scandal close to his door again, so soon after he had barely managed to avoid it with Georgiana? Would he condemn Charles' sister to the tragedy he had averted for his own? Caroline was silly and manipulative, but perhaps she would change in time. Surely he owed his friend that much.

Trapped, what other option was open to him? He sighed and turned to Caroline. His words, when they came, were forced out from between clenched teeth, giving them a taut, angry tone.

"Miss Bingley, will you allow your brother and me to discuss the details of our engagement. I trust you wish to marry?"

"Oh, Mr Darcy!" Caroline cried, with what might have been genuine delight. "Of course. Come, Annabelle, let us get some refreshments and allow the gentlemen to talk."

They had been gone but a moment when Charles let out a heavy sigh of relief.

"Well! I must confess I did not foresee those words coming out of your mouth."

"I did not intend on uttering them."

Charles' eyes narrowed.

"Come, Charles. You must have seen how that little performance was entirely engineered by your sister. Do you really think me foolish enough to attempt a seduction in a room full of people? Or a scoundrel enough to even countenance such behaviour?"

Charles shook his head, slowly.

"Then Caroline...?"

"Yes, Caroline," Darcy grumbled. "Still, I suppose she will make me no worse a wife than any other woman."

"She - she can be kind, Darcy. I know you will grow to care for her, if you do not at present." He sounded strangely sad, but Darcy was in no mood to placate his friend. It was for Charles' happiness he had sacrificed his own, what more did his friend desire?

"So you will marry her?" The slightest trace of doubt had crept into Charles' voice.

"I said as much, didn't I? Or do you intend to impugn my word now as well?" Darcy was already regretting his offer of marriage. Surely there would have been some other way out of it that did not mean his being bound to Caroline Bingley for life.

"Well, I'm glad," Charles said at last. He reached a hand out and clapped Darcy on the arm. "I could not wish for a better husband for my sister." He said nothing of there possibly existing, somewhere, a better wife for Darcy. "Let us not speak of specifics tonight, though." He eyed the crowd, who had begun to dart curious glances to their corner, one or two having spoken directly to Caroline and whose gazes were not curious, but knowing. "Surely now is the time for celebration?"

"Celebration," Darcy muttered, his eyes returning to his feet once more. How quickly everything had shifted. And how little he felt the need of celebrating such a change.

Chapter Seven

When Darcy woke to find himself safely in his London house, he felt a flare of relief, followed closely by anxiety. Was it a dream, or a memory played over as a dream? He threw off his covers, crossing the room to the window, and opening it, to breathe in the icy winter air. He forced himself into alertness and tried to retrace his last true memory. Caroline was there, yes, and Charles, too. But it had been a small gathering, not a ball. He felt a second, deep wave of relief. It was merely a dream that had him bound to marry Caroline Bingley.

I shall guard myself to avoid any dark corner she finds fit to go to, he thought, with a wry smile. Clearly, his sub-conscious mind thought as fondly of Caroline as his conscious self did, and credited her with quite as much cunning and manipulation.

What strange dreams are plaguing me tonight! he thought, closing the window and returning to his bed. His sheets were creased from much movement, and he felt scarcely rested at all. Still, he felt a resistance to clambering back into bed and attempting sleep a third time. *What nightmares wait for me now?* he thought, as he nonetheless smoothed his sheets and pulled them up to his chest. He stared up into the darkness and willed himself to stay awake, merely to wait for the dawn, which must surely arrive soon, and not risk his senses to dream again.

He was exhausted, though, and despite his intent, it was but a few moments before his lids grew heavy, and his thoughts gave way to oblivion once more...

Chapter Eight

The halls of Pemberley were colder than Darcy remembered, and it was not just a matter of temperature. Caroline Bingley - now Mrs Caroline Darcy - had terrified his staff into submission, so that there was no friendly banter between them, no whistling or murmured singing as a task was completed.

He was grateful for the solace of his study, yet lately, even that had felt less like a comfort and more like a prison cell to him. It was the one room he could call his own, for none but he would dare step inside, but the result of that was more and deeper isolation, rather than the sanctuary it had been in former times.

"Fitzwilliam!" He winced at the harsh tone of voice his wife applied to that name in particular. He had hoped, once married, that Caroline's edges would soften. If anything, they grated even more on his nerves, and he could not help but think of her with resentment.

"Fitzwilliam, darling!"

He gritted his teeth. As did her insistent use of his Christian name and any one of several endearments that were neither wanted nor encouraged. He had suggested that she might call him William, as Georgiana did, reminding her that Fitzwilliam was formal and rarely used by anyone with whom he shared any real intimacy. She had ignored the suggestion, insisting that Fitzwilliam was altogether more elegant and thus would be the name she used when they spoke to one another.

Realising he could hide no longer, unless he wished to continually be interrupted by her calling for him, he pulled the door of his study open and stepped into the corridor.

"Is something the matter?"

"Ah!" She beamed at him. "I wondered where you had got to. Do remember that my brother intends to call on us this afternoon. Why, is that what you intend on wearing?" She cast a critical eye over his clothing, and her lips turned down in disapproval.

"Must we wear our finery whenever friends call on us now?" he asked, irritated at the way she sought to control every element of his life, even that which had little importance.

"I am disappointed you do not think my brother worthy of the honour of a change of clothes." Caroline sniffed. "I know he is not quite so well-established as us -"

"Caroline -" Darcy held up a hand to stop her familiar tirade, and bowed, obediently. "If it is important to you then, of course, I will change." He could not bear to hear her hold forth yet again on the subject of their position in society, and how it compared or contrasted with the people they called friends. He had thought her obsession with rank would dissipate once they relocated from London to Pemberley, but, if anything, it had merely worsened.

"Is Georgiana at home?"

"Georgiana?" Caroline feigned ignorance, but Darcy was not deceived. He sighed.

"Tell me you two have not had another of your disagreements?" If he, himself, found Caroline difficult to manage, Georgiana found her barely tolerable, an opinion she was not shy about sharing. He felt the burden of unending battle settle over his shoulders like a weight. He had thought the two ladies well enough acquainted before the announcement of his marriage reached Georgiana's ears: in fact, he had even presumed them to be friends, or disposed to be so. Georgiana had seemed amiable to Caroline when they had met in the past, and Caroline claimed to find Georgiana utterly enchanting. In fact, she had gone out of her way to enquire after Darcy's sister in the weeks before their engagement, as if the two were fond friends and naturally curious about one another. Once the wedding had taken place, however, it was as if both ladies had undergone a complete transformation. Caroline strove always to come out on top in Darcy's affection, an effort which was largely fruitless, for he could not quite forgive her for the manner in which they became engaged in the first place, nor had she ever succeeded in truly winning his heart. She guarded her position as mistress of Pemberley jealously and used every opportunity afforded her to attack Georgiana, disguising her thrusts behind smiles and words of encouragement. Darcy knew she was counting the days until his sister was married off and out of their hair, and as such, continued to push Georgiana towards matches he, himself, despaired of. He was more than ever pitched on the side of his sister, determined that she would not be forced to make the same mistakes he had and would marry a good man whose chief concern was her happiness. He might have considered Bingley agreeable enough to the task, were it not for Charles' sudden and regrettable marriage to Annabelle Parker, one week after his and Caroline's own wedding. His friend's marriage at least appeared a little happier than Darcy's, although whether that was because Charles was better resigned to his fate than Darcy or his wife a little more agreeable than Caroline regularly made an effort to be, he could not say.

"Georgiana is out," Caroline said, with a shrug of her shoulders. "She would not say where she was going or when she would be back. I, at least, insisted upon her taking her companion with her."

This companion was a new initiative of Caroline's, instituted in an attempt to keep watch on Georgiana when companionship with Caroline directly seemed unpalatable to Darcy's sister. The maid was retained under Caroline's name, although she was despatched at Georgiana's bidding. Darcy knew, and fancied his sister was only too aware, that the maid reported back on her movements directly to Caroline, and as such, she had well practised the art of dodging her maid at any opportunity that she wanted a little privacy. Darcy frowned. Word that the two ladies had gone out together was of little comfort to him. Who knew what mischief Georgiana might fall into with such a companion? Caroline seemed to care little, in fact, she almost seemed to relish the thought of Georgiana suffering some catastrophe, and he wondered if her insistence on having Georgiana's every move observed was designed to push her into behaviour she would otherwise not have considered.

"She will be sorry to miss Charles, in any case," Darcy offered, as a parting shot before taking his leave to change. "She is very fond of your brother, and of Mrs Bingley."

Annabelle Bingley was an afterthought, for she was firmly Caroline's friend, and thus of little consequence to Georgiana.

But Charles was a second brother to her, and someone she would turn to for advice more readily than she would to Darcy of late. The realisation hurt him, though he would not own it.

"Perhaps she will return before they leave. They are staying for dinner, are not they?"

Caroline's response was but a sniff, and Darcy took it as a dismissal, hurrying to change and return in good time for the arrival of their guests.

"CHARLES! HOW WONDERFUL to see you. Annabelle, I do hope you aren't sickening for anything. You look a little flushed." Caroline had voiced this last with the utmost concern, yet Darcy knew his wife well enough to recognise the hint of an insult nestled amidst her professed fear for her friend. Ignoring her, he reached for Charles' hand, grasping it warmly.

"It is good to see you again, Charles. How do you find Derbyshire?"

"Beautiful," Bingley said, with a brief glance towards his sister. "At least, what we have seen of it is pleasant to look at. We have not had so much time for walking and exploring as I might have hoped."

Annabelle sniffed, and tossed her hair, turning her attention pointedly away from her husband and towards his sister.

"Caroline, dear, you look so different with your hair pinned so. Almost matronly!"

The ladies fell to discussing the friends they shared, sharpening their cruel tongues on shared enemies rather than on one another, and Darcy felt free to speak to his own friend unhindered by the ears of his wife.

"I hope you will take full advantage of the grounds while you are here, in that case." He smiled. "We might walk, or ride, as you wish. If we are lucky we might even see our way to some shooting, assuming the ladies are content to allow us our freedom."

"We would happily free you to undertake such a pastime if it would release us from having to look interested," Caroline said. "Besides, Annabelle and I have plenty to occupy us here. Perhaps my dear husband will permit me to organise a small soiree, for I would dearly like to introduce you to my friends." Darcy was not given a chance to agree or disagree with this request, for it was spoken as a matter of fact, as if Caroline had already determined what she would do, regardless of Darcy's approval. "The new Lady Frobisher, you know, has an estate not far from here, and we are very good friends. She is an emigree, you know," Caroline's voice dropped to a pseudo-whisper. "From France. Dreadfully elegant, but so severe! Still, her sense of style is exquisite, and she never fails to compliment me on my own attention to fashion and detail." Caroline lifted her chin, intent on demonstrating the particular sparkle of a pair of ear-bobs that had been a recent gift from Darcy to his wife. A gift of duty rather than any real affection, for Caroline had been none too reserved when it came to suggesting notions she most admired and wished for. Plagued with guilt for the sharp words Darcy often spoke to his wife, which were bred out of his own hatred of his current circumstances, he was all too inclined to attempt to repair the damage with such a purchase, yet he had not yet managed to buy his way into a happier marriage, and lately began to wonder if such a feat were indeed possible.

"You are as kind as ever, sister, to befriend someone leaving behind such suffering," Charles said, with a small smile towards Caroline that, Darcy noticed, was not returned. In fact, he wondered if Caroline had even heard her brother's compliment.

"Your estate is so vast, Mr Darcy," Annabelle said, breaking away from Caroline's hypnotic monologue long enough to pay her host a genuine compliment. "I had no idea Pemberley so grand a place!"

"No idea!" Caroline laughed, but the sound was not a pleasant one. "Really, Annabelle, you tease us. Pemberley is well regarded throughout England as one of the prettiest of all the country estates."

"Now, Caroline, I don't think that is altogether accurate -" Darcy began, disliking the superior tone Caroline slipped into when discussing their home as if she had had some role to play in its flourishing. That Pemberley existed at all, and thrived as it did, was largely down to the careful work of his father. Old Mr Darcy had invested well and run his estate wisely, taking good care of his tenants and in return earning their respect and devotion. Darcy strove to emulate his father, yet Caroline seemed to give little credence to the importance of giving due care and consideration to the managing of such an estate. She merely enjoyed the benefits afforded such a home and had already successfully encouraged Darcy to host two large-scale parties this season. She was angling for a third, and it seemed the arrival of Charles and Annabelle Bingley were just the excuse she had been hoping for to hasten her plans.

"I mean - it is so very different from London," Annabelle hurried out, eager not to upset her hots so soon after arriving. "So green, and pleasant."

"Indeed!" Caroline nodded, accepting this comment as an adequate explanation and forgiving her friend for the perceived slight in her earlier comment. "It is far pleasanter than London! I do not know how you can bear to live there so much. Surely, Charles, you are eager to take a house in the country again, for you were so happy at Netherfield."

The silence that swept over the room was so sudden and complete that even Darcy was surprised by its fervency. He noticed Caroline's cheeks drain of all colour as she realised her mistake.

"Happy, yes." Charles cleared his throat. "But that was a long time ago. Everything is different now, is it not?" He turned his attention to the piano. "Do you still have much opportunity to play, sister? Or does the provision of music all fall on Georgiana's shoulders?" He lifted his gaze to Darcy's. "Where is your sister, Darcy? I hope she is not avoiding us?"

"Avoiding? Not at all." Darcy smiled, grateful for the interest his friend showed in the absent Georgiana. "She had a few tasks to see to, I believe, but will return and join us for dinner. And you will stay here a few days yet, so you are bound to be afforded the chance to hear her playing. She continues to improve, if it were possible."

"Yes, we can hardly pry her fingers from the keys," Caroline remarked, with a pinched smile. "How pleasant it is to have an hour of silence, without her trilling through scale after scale. Annabelle, come and take a turn about the room with me, for you must be in need of some exercise after your long journey..."

Chapter Nine

"Was this not worth rising early?" Darcy asked as he and Charles slowed their horses to a walk the next morning. They had planned to go out at first light, seizing the opportunity for a morning ride without the interference of any of the ladies at Pemberley, and seeking not to disturb them with their early morning activities. As it was, his friend had been bleary-eyed and uncharacteristically quiet on meeting. A quick ride had blown the sleep from Darcy's brains, and he could only hope the same was true for Charles.

"What fine countryside!" Charles said, looking around at the green expanses and the grey hills that could be seen in the distance. "It does me good to see it! Do you know, I have not had such exercise since before we returned to London?" He shook his head, marvelling at the fact. "And how I have missed it!"

"In that case, you must ride just as often as you wish to, while you are here," Darcy said, turning his horse and beginning to retrace their route back towards the house.

"Might we ride on a little further?" Bingley asked. "That is, you do not have any pressing desire to return just at present?"

"We can stay out as long as you wish. The ladies are well catered for and will be quite content to breakfast without us, I don't doubt."

Charles smiled, and they rode on in silence for a few moments, before he spoke again.

"It is good of you to host us, Darcy, and at such short notice."

"Was it so very short?" Darcy shook his head. "There is no such thing, surely, when one visits family."

"Nonetheless..." Charles trailed off, and Darcy was left wondering what lay behind the sad smile that lingered on his friend's features, or the quietness that seemed so uncharacteristic of Charles Bingley yet had become his apparent norm since his arrival at Pemberley.

"I wished to leave London," he said, at length. "That is, I rather *had* to leave London."

"I have warned you about those card tables..." Darcy remarked, drily. He bit back his attempt at humour when he saw the deep flush that tainted his friend's cheeks.

"You see, I knew there was little point in attempting to deceive you. You know me too well and could surely tell at first glance that financially...we are not...that is, I -" He trailed off.

"Have you come into difficulty?" Darcy asked, his voice gruff in an attempt to extract the truth from his friend whilst sparing his pride.

"Not exactly." Charles' voice was flat. "That would suggest some accident of fate. I rather think my wife..." he shook his head. "I ought not to speak so. And yet how can I be anything but truthful with my oldest friend? The truth of the matter is that Annabelle has little concept of money or how quickly it might be spent, particularly in London." He sighed. "You know I am no miser, Darcy, nor have I ever wanted for much, thank heavens. But even I can see her extravagance lacks wisdom and foresight." When he lifted his gaze to Darcy's his features were miserable. "I sometimes think she is intent on bankrupting me. If we stay in London it is certainly a very real possibility!"

Had it been anyone other than Bingley, Darcy would have laughed, and advised the fellow to keep a tighter grip on his purse strings, but Charles looked so miserable that Darcy knew any reproach, however lightly offered or genuinely meant would hit his friend too hard.

"Then do not stay in London."

Bingley frowned.

"I am not sure I can afford to remove, at present."

"Stay here." Darcy warmed to the idea as soon as it was spoken. "You know you are welcome to stay as long as you wish it. Surely Annabelle would benefit from having companions under the same roof, and I assure you I would be more than grateful to have you stay."

His fervent encouragement had caused Bingley to frown, reading some deeper motivation behind Darcy's invitation, which he hurried to negate.

"Stay here. What trouble can she get up to in the country?"

"With nothing to do she will drive us both to distraction. She is not fond of walking nor of reading nor any quiet pastime. At least in London, there are exhibitions and concerts and any number of friends to see. Or perhaps, if I am clever, I might persuade her towards Bath. One can be extravagant at far less cost in Bath..."

They fell silent, and Darcy resigned himself to raising the issue again later, once his friend had had time to consider his options further. He did not like to admit how much he already dreaded Bingley leaving, and being left alone once more in his home with just his wife and sister for company. It was ironic, he thought, with a grimace, that what had once been a dream for him had become a trial.

"Bath is so far away, Charles. Why not at least stay here a little longer. Caroline will be happy to have you, and Annabelle too."

"Georgiana."

Darcy raised his eyes.

"Yes, Georgiana too."

"No." Bingley nodded in the direction he had been looking. "Georgiana."

Darcy followed his gaze, his eyebrows drawing together in a frown.

"Georgiana."

The shadow was a little far off, but Darcy would have recognised the slight figure of his sister anywhere. What struck him as incongruous was seeing her *here*. They were still near the boundary of Pemberley - too far for a brief morning stroll. Georgiana must be here with a purpose, then. *Has there been some accident?* Darcy was reluctant to startle his sister, who seemed to intent on her purpose as to have not noticed the two gentlemen at present. He slid off his horse, handing the reins to Charles, and jogged to meet her.

"Georgie!" he called.

At the sound of his voice, she started, glancing up almost guiltily. Upon recognising first him and then Charles, however, the startled, trapped look fled and was replaced with something altogether different. This was the face he had come to silently refer to as the *new Georgiana*, both like and unlike his young sister that it quite unnerved him. This was the Georgiana who engaged in verbal sparring with Caroline across the dinner table, avoided his company whenever he made the suggestion of them spending time together, and seemed to almost enjoy looking for opportunities to torment him.

"Is anything the matter?" he asked, determined to retain the upper hand. After all, of the two of them, he had the most reason to be there.

"No," she said, innocently. "Ought there to be?"

"It is quite a distance from the house," Darcy said, patiently. "And very early. I hope Charles and I did not disturb you upon our departure."

"I hardly noticed you at all." There, that was a cutting tone of voice she had surely learned from her sister-in-law. Darcy shook off the barb, unwilling to let her know how her dismissive toss of the head hurt him. Despite the difference in their ages, they had always been close, perhaps because of the shared loss of their parents. The affair with Wickham had originally seemed to bring them closer, but no, that must have been fancy on his part, for this Georgiana was like a stranger to him.

"Well, would you like to join us?"

She arched an eyebrow.

"Riding and shooting and discussing matters of business?" she snorted. "I'd rather not, thank you."

"Then perhaps we might accompany you back to Pemberley?" This suggestion came from over Darcy's shoulder, and he noticed that Charles had likewise dismounted his horse, and towed them both. "What say you, Darcy? Are you about ready for breakfast?"

"Breakfast!" Georgiana turned away from Darcy altogether, offering a dazzling smile to his friend. "Well, Mr Bingley, that is a splendid idea, I must say. I shall certainly allow *you* to accompany me back. Perhaps my brother can see to the horses."

Both gentlemen exchanged glances, and Darcy saw his own confusion reflected in Charles' features. Nonetheless, after a moment of hesitation, his friend acquiesced and offered Georgiana his arm. She took it without an ounce of shyness, and instead began to speak quite familiarly to Charles Bingley as if he were *her* friend, and not her brother's. It would almost be improper, but for the fact that the gentleman in question was Charles Bingley, and newly married. Surely Georgiana was merely trying to prove a point, to goad her brother into some reaction. He refused to rise to it but obediently followed the couple down the hill with both horses in tow.

I cannot help but think my choice of a wife was an equally unsuccessful a choice for a sister, as far as Georgiana was concerned. His thoughts flared before him, featuring another life, walking behind Georgiana once more, but this time seeing her arm in arm with a young lady with dark hair and bright eyes. The two chattered on happily as if they were close friends, and in this version of reality, Darcy did not mind being forgotten, left to trail behind the two ladies. He blinked, and the image was gone. *Will I always be haunted by Elizabeth Bennet?* he thought, as the party wound slowly back towards Pemberley.

CAROLINE WAS YET TO surface, and Annabelle, too, preferred to sleep late, and so it was a quiet table at breakfast that morning, seating only Charles, Darcy and Georgiana at almost equidistant places along the large table. Darcy had intended on sitting at one corner, for the three to enjoy a quiet meal. Instead, Georgiana had quite presumptuously moved to be closer to Charles in an effort, Darcy felt certain, to exclude him. He ought not to mind it, for truly it was some relief to see his sister willingly engaging in conversation, and to see Charles begin to emerge from the shell he had sunk into many months previously.

What he did not like was the pointed smiles and teasing comments that seemed so foreign coming out of Georgiana's lips, and directed at Charles, who she knew to be married. If it were not so bewildering to him he would have made some attempt to end the conversation or to take Georgiana to task, but what could he say? She had been careful in her choices so that he could hold no particular comment or exchange up as particularly flirtatious or ill-advised, yet he was certain that was her intent.

If Charles noticed anything amiss he did not say as much, nor play along to any great degree with Georgiana's flights of fancy. In fact, he acted every inch the gentleman, striving at every opportunity to involve Darcy in their discussion, to lead Georgiana back to topics that were more befitting the breakfast table. In short, he acted entirely as he should, and Darcy was grateful for him.

"Mr Bingley, if you wish to truly see all that is best and most beautiful about Pemberley, you must allow me to map out a walk for you this afternoon," Georgiana said, with a dismissive toss of her head in Darcy's direction. "My brother has hardly been here, and so I am sure his information is not current: nor has he ever been fond of doing anything for pleasure alone. But you are here for a visit, and you must want to enjoy yourself, so I will show you the most pleasant places to walk."

"You are very kind, Miss Georgiana. I am sure my wife will be eager to see all that Pemberley has to offer -"

"Oh," Georgiana sighed, extravagantly. "Yes, of course, Mrs Bingley might accompany us, should she wish to, only -" she paused and dropped her gaze. "I do so want to do it today and, well, she has yet to emerge." She let out a light, musical laugh that sounded dangerous to Darcy's ears. "She will have to hurry up and join us or I might steal you away!"

"I am sure she will not be long," Bingley said, a little uncertainly. "And Caroline, too, will doubtless want to spend time with us. I have spoken to her little of late and am eager to know how she is settled here."

"Do you not write?" Georgiana asked, innocently. "I know *some* brothers are wont to write often, always wanting to check up on their sisters in their absence, and ensure they are behaving as a properly brought up young lady ought to, and remaining closeted away from the world and other people lest they involve themselves in something scandalous -" she stopped speaking, suddenly, and changed tack. Her voice became altogether gentler. "I am sure *you* put full trust in *your* sister, Mr Bingley. How kind a brother you must have been to her, over the years."

Bingley said nothing but focused with all his energy on the consumption of his breakfast.

"Georgiana." Darcy cleared his throat. It took a second utterance of her name before she designed to look up at him, and fixed him with a glare so intense that he felt shocked to his core. "I must speak with you a moment. Would you be so good as to step out into the hallway?"

"And leave our guest alone? Poor show, William!"

"I do not mind it!" Bingley said, hurriedly. "In fact - perhaps I ought to be the one to leave. Yes, I think - I think I will go and see if Annabelle might be persuaded to rise and join us on the walk you mentioned Miss - ah - Miss Georgiana." He had hurried to his feet as he spoke and was halfway out of the door before he had even finished his sentence.

"That was rude," Georgiana said, after a moment of icy silence had descended over the table.

"I fancy poor Bingley wanted a moment to himself," Darcy remarked, drily. "You ought not to hang on him like that, Georgiana. It is not becoming."

"And that is, of course, my aim in life. To be *becoming* in the opinion of my brother." Georgiana had muttered this, half under her breath, yet Darcy caught every word.

"Must we always be at odds with one another these days, Georgie? We did not always fight like this. I thought -"

"You thought that I might stay your sweet-tempered little sister forever, never forming my own opinions or having my own wishes or plans for my life? That I might eagerly follow in your footsteps, and choose a miserable life married to a person I despise merely that I might *appear* content and avoid a scandal?"

Georgiana pushed her chair back, noisily, from the table and stood, gaining energy as she spoke.

"I never blamed you for parting me and Wickham. In fact, I spent much of the time after that blaming myself for the tangle, thinking I ought to have known better, ought not to have been so easily led. I thought *you* blamed me too, and had determined to avoid me because you could not stand to look at me. Then I discover that you have hurried into a marriage with a woman you made no attempt to hide your disdain for on account of some misplaced sense of propriety!" She laughed, a harsh, angry sound that made Darcy recoil. "We all see how miserable it has made you - and how miserable *you* have made the rest of the people that live here by bringing Caroline Bingley as your wife. If this is the future I have to look forward to by being *becoming* and proper you may keep it, brother. I have no intention of sacrificing my happiness!"

With a look towards him that was pure loathing, Georgiana stormed out of the room, pulling the door closed behind her with a slam.

Chapter Ten

The slam of the door ended Darcy's dream in an instant and jerked him back to the present. He was in his bed again - his own bed, in the London town-house, not Pemberley - and alone, not surrounded by guests.

This time he wished for light, for he had failed to chase the spectres of his dreams away. He reached, with shaking hand, for a candle and with some difficulty lit it. The dark receded, just a fraction, taking with it the immediate effects of this last dream. Did Georgiana really hate him so very much, or was this a shadow-sister, a version of her that his subconscious had created to torment him? And to what end?

He ran a hand through his hair and willed his heart-rate to slow. A glance at the fob-watch which sat on the low table by his bed told him it had been but a few hours in all since he had first arrived home that evening, yet he had travelled miles and months in dreams. He felt as if the world as he knew it had spun on its axis. Elizabeth deceived by Wickham. Himself forced into marrying Caroline Bingley - and surely the dreadful vision of Pemberley was only a foretaste of what the future held in store for him if he ever did make so foolish a decision as to marry a woman he could barely stand. And Bingley! Entrapped into a marriage with a woman so unequal to him in character that she sought to ruin him. Darcy frowned. The Annabelle Parker of his dream had been Bingley's equal in social standing and background, yet his friend was miserable. It might have been fantasy only, but surely some truth was there, hidden in plain sight if only he could deduce it.

Everything stemmed from his decision to leave Hertfordshire: to separate Bingley from Jane Bennet. If they had stayed in Hertfordshire, Bingley would likely be well on the way to reaching an agreement. He might be able to warn Elizabeth Bennet about Wickham's true nature - yet why did he feel the need?

"I would not want any young lady to fall victim to George Wickham," he murmured aloud. Yet even that was not the true root of his unhappiness. He had felt that far earlier in the dream: when dream-Elizabeth had spoken so cuttingly of *him*. If her true opinion of him was anything close to the one the spectral version of her had expressed then he would be sorry indeed. He was not perfect, but did he truly deserve so harsh an assessment?

"Yes," he acknowledged, falling back against his pillow. "Yes, and again yes." He had acted proudly and unjustly towards her and towards her family, and had no excuse to offer. He had thought himself better than her - better than almost everyone he came across in Hertfordshire, whereas Bingley had been pleasant and agreeable to all, seeing friends and potential family where Darcy saw only those who would ingratiate themselves for their own ends. And when had Elizabeth Bennet ever sought to ingratiate herself with him? If anything, she did the opposite: and was pitched to do everything in her power to rile him. Yet now...he almost felt as if he missed her combative spirit. How dreary it was to be faced with simpering Annabelle Parkers or snide Caroline Bingleys for companionship, who offered no opinion save for a reflection of his own, and could offer no wit or humour to a conversation that was not merely the repetition of unkind gossip.

And Jane Bennet! How could he have been so convinced of her cunning? She was no Caroline Bingley, and it was plain from one glance, had he ever truly spared it, that the affections Charles felt for Jane Bennet were returned in full, if concealed, as spoke of her good character.

Sleep eluded him then, and he knew he would not return to it that evening. He threw off his bedclothes and moved to stand, fumbling in the shadowy dark for a robe, which he pulled on as a barrier to the biting winter air.

I must think. He paced as he thought, feeling with every step the solid ground beneath his feet, with every brisk lungful of cold air how glad he was to be present in this reality, and able to prevent the potential futures spelt out in dreams from coming to pass.

There is but one solution, and I can only hope it is not too late.

He went to the window, throwing open the drapes and squinting out into the darkness. Dawn would not be for some hours yet.

Well, then I will wait for the dawn. And as soon as it is light, I will set my plan in motion...

Chapter Eleven

"You wish to return to Hertfordshire?"

It was still early when Darcy called on Charles and Caroline, yet fortunately, they were both at breakfast and welcomed him to join them. He had taken a cup of tea, but no food, for he was anxious and could not countenance a morsel of food until he had spoken his plan to them and gained their agreement. Well, Charles' agreement. He felt certain his friend would be only too happy to return with him, in spite of whatever protest Caroline was certain to mount.

"But we have only just left that dreary place!" she began, her voice already taking on a whining tone which might have been more effective, had it not been muffled by chewing.

"We left too hastily, too quickly. Surely you agree, Charles?"

"Well..."

Charles glanced at Caroline for confirmation, but Darcy commanded his attention.

"You left because we told you we must, and for that I am sorry. I confess it was not without art. I and -" he paused, wondering what would be gained him by incriminating Charles' sister in the scheme, however much her actions had set it in motion. He still smarted from the memory of dream-Georgiana pitched so adamantly against him, and could not bring himself to upset the union of another brother and sister merely to ease the burden of guilt on himself.

"I made the decision," he said, quickly glancing at Caroline, and away again, for she was looking at him with a combination of confusion, horror and fury that he could not bear to witness. "For reasons I must confess now were utterly wrong-headed. I wished to remove you from the influence of those I thought intended you harm. I see now how utterly misguided I was."

"*Those who intended me harm?*" Charles quoted his own words back to him. "Dear me, Darcy, do I have so very many enemies?"

"No," he said, honestly. "It is far worse. You have friends who think they know what is in your best interests." Bowing his head slightly, he hurried out a muddled confession of his intention to separate Charles from Jane Bennet, on account of his suspicion that she sought to entrap him into marriage. "I felt certain she did not care for you - could not possibly match your feelings for her - and rather wished to wed you for your wealth instead of any real affection. You are the finest fellow I know, Charles, and deserve more than that from your marriage."

"You deduced all this from observing us at a dance?"

"My own observation and overhearing an unfortunate comment from another guest." Darcy grimaced. "Eavesdropping has never yet worked in my favour, either overhearing or being overheard. I hereby resign from it entirely. But I confess I was goaded into action on account of hearsay, and upon reflection, I think it entirely misguided."

"And what has occurred to change your mind so abruptly and completely?"

Caroline Bingley had found her voice at last, setting down her meal to regard Darcy with a glare.

"Has Jane Bennet written to you directly to implore you to return my brother to her clutches?"

"Caroline!" Bingley was shocked to hear such an unkind assessment fall from his sister's lips, and Darcy was amused to see the shade of red that Caroline turned as she attempted to control her anger.

"I have received no letters," Darcy admitted. "But I did have an unsettled night." He had considered telling all about his dreams, and had even set them down on paper so that he might remember the details that most caused him to repent and change his views. As the sun rose and he read through the notes once more he thought better of the plan, however, fearing his friend would think him gone mad or turned a drunkard. He had stowed the notes safely in his case, and instead constructed a simpler explanation for his change of heart.

"I was awake with the dawn, reflecting on our decision to leave and the evening that precipitated it, and I was forced to acknowledge that I acted in haste and with good intentions but altogether unnecessarily. We were happy at Hertfordshire, were we not? And Netherfield is still yours for a time. Why not return there, and enjoy Christmas as we originally intended, with riding and shooting and peace and quiet."

As if to illustrate his point, a carriage rattled down the street outside, and the noise of a shout broke through the quiet of the breakfast table.

"I see your true intention," Bingley said, at length, in a tone of voice that was either annoyed or amused, Darcy could not quite tell which. "You merely wish to avoid being forced to attend any more parties this Christmas!"

Darcy laughed, feeling that with that one comment his battle was won.

"You are right, Charles. Give me solitude, that is the one gift I ask for, this festive tide."

"Pemberley!" Caroline screeched at last.

Both gentlemen turned to look at her.

"If you desire solitude then why not remove to Pemberley? There you might have it all! Peace and quiet. Land to roam in. And Georgiana, dear Georgiana. She will be most content to meet you, will she not?"

"My sister is not at Pemberley at present," Darcy said, calmly. "She has been lately calling on my aunt in Kent, and I have taken the liberty of writing to invite her to join us at Netherfield." He pulled a note from his pocket and consulted Charles with a raised eyebrow. "If you do not mind it?"

"Of course not!" Charles beamed. "Yes, indeed, she must come. Will she have time to travel and be with us for Christmas?"

"I shall send this straight away and do not doubt she will be with us before very long at all." His smile was genuine. "She has been agitating to come to Hertfordshire since first hearing we were there, and it is so long since we have spent any time together."

"Then we must make haste and hurry back ahead of her!" Charles said, throwing his napkin into the air in celebration. "Are you packed, Darcy? Come, Caroline! We must gather our belongings. I cannot wait to see the look of astonishment on Miss Bennet's face when we call on her! She will imagine us gone and then surprise! We shall appear again. What a fine time we shall have all together for Christmas."

DARCY FELT A WEIGHT lift from his shoulders as the busyness of London gave way to the rolling green countryside of Hertfordshire. He was doing the right thing, he felt sure, despite the showdown with Caroline Bingley that had occurred moments before they left. He grimaced, recalling the way she had railed at both he and Charles for their insistence on returning to Netherfield immediately.

"Well, I certainly do not intend on joining you!" she cried, with a toss of her glossy head. "How can you dream of uprooting so close to Christmas? And trading all that London has to offer for...Hertfordshire." Her words had dripped with disdain.

"Caroline, dear, you know Darcy is not fond of London society at the best of times, and I confess even I would prefer a little peace and quiet this year!" Charles had attempted to placate his sister in promising to throw another party upon their return or perhaps inviting some particular friends of hers to accompany them to Netherfield for the festivities. Both of these suggestions had been met with a dismissive snort, and eventually, even Charles' sanguine temper had begun to fray. "Well, Caroline I am sorry to part with you, and I shan't make you come with us, but I certainly do not intend to stay here and be miserable all Christmas. The house is plenty populated enough to credit your staying alone, and I am sure you will find adequate company amongst our friends and family. We might reunite in the new year if you see fit to return to Netherfield. As it stands, it is the property I have taken and I ought not to leave it uninhabited for so long a stretch."

Even Darcy had been surprised to see Charles so firmly sticking to his guns, and fancied that, had he not been beside him, had the very suggestion of returning to Hertfordshire not been suggested and encouraged by him, that Bingley may well have folded under the opposition of his sister.

Speed, then, became of the essence, for to delay would mean capitulation. Hurrying Charles into the carriage, they had departed London before the hour was out, and both men had fallen into companionable quiet, each watching the passing of the scenery and nursing his own thoughts.

"Jolly good plan, this, Darcy," Charles remarked, as they reached what could definitely be referred to as Hertfordshire. "Never did care for London much. I wouldn't have gone in the first place, had Caroline not concocted some spurious reason for our immediate return."

"Oh?" Darcy turned. He had never known what Charles' reasons for beating a hasty retreat to London had been, only been reassured by Caroline that his heart was set on departing, and being only too happy to facilitate the move, if it meant preventing what he had thought of as a very unwise match between his friend and Jane Bennet.

"She claimed Uncle Edward was unwell and wrote to request our company." He laughed. "Poor fellow has never been fitter in his life, and whilst he was thrilled to see us and welcomed us with open arms certainly had never written demanding we visit." He shook his head. "My sister is altogether too fond of an opportune falsehood if it secures her will being done. I don't mind telling you it is not a trait that is becoming."

He paused. "Don't say as much to anyone, though, will you Darcy? You know I think aloud when I talk to you. I oughtn't to speak so freely about my sister."

"I shall say nothing of it," Darcy promised, feeling somewhat convicted by his own role in Charles' rapid relocation.

"I certainly was surprised to see you so determined to accompany us!" Bingley paused, his pleasant features folding into a frown. "I hope you were not unhappy at Netherfield."

"Tis on my account we return there now, is not it?" Darcy asked, with a sly grin.

"Right! Indeed it is." Charles smiled happily. "Then I can only imagine you returned to London in support of me, and for that I thank you. It credits me with still more evidence of what a great friend you are."

Darcy groaned, low in his throat. He did not feel a great friend: for, intentional or otherwise, he had been complicit in creating this situation, and if his dreams were as prophetic as they had felt to him that morning, he would not consider himself a friend to Charles Bingley until he managed, somehow, to right the wrong.

"Look! Who are those ladies walking, do you think/"

Darcy felt a strange certainty, even before Bingley spoke again, that he knew precisely who at least one of the figures would be, and did not need to look to confirm his suspicions. Indeed, it was almost precisely the moment he thought of her that his friend spoke the name aloud.

"Why it is Miss Bennet! Miss Elizabeth Bennet, at any rate, and another lady I do not recognise. Here, Darcy, shall we not slow the carriage and see if we might be of some service to them?"

"Perhaps - perhaps they would prefer to walk," Darcy said, feeling his courage fail now that he was faced with the spectre of Elizabeth Bennet in the flesh once more. He could remember all too clearly the anger of her words when she discussed him with Mr Wickham and forced himself to recall that he had no knowledge if she had ever actually spoken thus. *It was a dream, nothing more.* Even so, he did not relish the thought of seeing her again, so suddenly, and yet it was his own hand, not Bingley's, that lowered the carriage window, and his own voice that hailed the two figures, almost before he was even aware of doing so.

"Miss Elizabeth! Good afternoon!"

"Mr Darcy?"

Darcy was quite certain that he had never seen Elizabeth Bennet so discomposed as she appeared at that moment. No, not even when she traipsed into Netherfield with six inches of mud coating her petticoat and demanded, soaked to the skin and breathless from exertion, to see her sister. Even then she had maintained her poise, the utter confidence she seemed to exude even surrounded by other people at a ball when he himself felt so out of his depth. Now, though, she was surprised, and he found himself smiling, amused to see the effect of such an emotion on her dainty features, the way her dark eyes widened in acknowledgement of the carriage and the two gentlemen it contained.

"And Mr Bingley? Surely - I believed you had gone to London?"

"Indeed, we did!" Bingley laughed. "Here, let us stop a moment." The carriage had slowed with the wordless instruction of a thump on the roof, and now the driver slowed further, to a stop.

"And what, you found it wanting for excitement?" Elizabeth's eyes sparkled, and she was herself once more, in control and poised to answer any observation with humour. Darcy felt the amused smile slip off his features and struggled to remain impassive.

"Alas, it possessed rather too much excitement for Darcy and myself." Bingley beamed. "And so we are retreating to Netherfield where we might enjoy some peace and quiet." He paused. "Yet it is providential we should be passing at the very moment you are taking a walk. Here, might we offer you a ride back to Longbourn? It is on our way, after all."

"You are very kind, Mr Bingley." Elizabeth shared a glance with the lady beside her, and then lifted her eyes to Darcy's in a look that might have been a challenge. "I would not wish to inconvenience you, or Mr Darcy."

"What inconvenience?" Bingley brushed off the suggestion. "We have a carriage with two spare seats, and you are two ladies. We might make a comfortable end to our journey and save you a mile's walk."

Another moment's polite hesitation and the ladies were conveyed into the carriage.

"You must permit me to introduce my aunt, Mrs Gardiner," Elizabeth said, a little breathless from the exertion of first walking and then clambering into the carriage. Both gentlemen greeted Mrs Gardiner with a smile, and she glanced knowingly at Bingley for a moment before training her pale eyes on Darcy.

"Mr Darcy...." She turned his name over as if probing it for recognition. "I cannot imagine you to be the same Mr Darcy who resides most often at Pemberley?"

"Indeed he is!" Bingley offered, jumping in before Darcy had a chance to formulate a response. "See, Darcy, your reputation precedes you, even to the aunts and uncles of those we might call friends."

Everybody laughed, politely, even though Charles' joke was not particularly funny.

Mrs Gardiner recounted her childhood in Derbyshire, and in the short journey back to Longbourn it became apparent that she and Darcy shared more than one or two acquaintances in common.

"What a small world we live in!" she marvelled, as Darcy helped her down from the carriage. Depositing her safely, Darcy turned to offer a helping hand to Elizabeth, and their eyes met, briefly. She was regarding him curiously, as if she were not quite sure she recognised him. The thought was strangely unsettling. *Have I changed so much in our short separation?* He was not sure whether this was something to lament, or to rejoice over.

Chapter Twelve

Upon reaching Longbourn, there could be no question of the two gentlemen not being pressed into taking tea with the family - indeed, Mrs Bennet did not stop rejoicing over their sudden and surprising return long enough to allow either man to speak a word.

Elizabeth sidled to the back of the parlour, allowing Mrs Bennet full sway in interrogating first Mr Darcy and then Mr Bingley, who bore her inquisition with rather more grace and good humour than his friend.

"We just happened to be passing," he explained. "When we saw Mrs Gardiner and Miss Elizabeth out walking we could not conceive of leaving them to continue on foot when we had half a carriage to spare."

"But how came you to be passing?" Mrs Bennet pressed, glancing back at Elizabeth as if her daughter might possess the answer neither gentleman had yet offered. "We were quite convinced of your absenting yourselves to London for Christmas - yes, and very disappointed we were, too, by this turn of events, were not we, Lizzy?"

"Devastated," Elizabeth confirmed.

"Where is Jane?" Mrs Bennet recalled the absence of her eldest daughter almost immediately and dispatched Kitty to fetch her from upstairs. "She will want to see you, of course, Mr Bingley," she said, quickly. "Please, do sit down, both of you, and I shall fetch us some tea." Lydia was ordered to arrange for some refreshments, which chore she undertook with rather less grace than her sister.

"Miss Elizabeth, I hope your sister rallies?"

Lizzy had been so distracted by the chaos of Longbourn's parlour - rendered still more chaotic by the addition of both gentlemen as well as her aunt and uncle - that she had scarcely noticed Mr Darcy's sidestepping the crowd and finding himself in the corner to her right.

"Rallies?" she smiled. "I was not aware she needed to, sir."

"Ah, indeed." His black eyebrows furrowed. "Forgive me, I was under the impression she was unwell."

"Not at all," Elizabeth said, arching an eyebrow.

"And you - that is, you all - are you all quite well?" Darcy continued, after a moment's awkward pause in their exchange.

"Indeed we are, Mr Darcy." Elizabeth struggled to contain her amusement. The poor man looked pained, as if straining to conjure conversation was the most difficult task he could conceive of. Elizabeth decided to take pity on him and turned their exchange once more to their surprising return to Hertfordshire. She had not yet determined the true reason for their return, which had, it seemed to her, mirrored their equally swift departure. "I see Miss Bingley is not with you. Has she gone on ahead to Netherfield, Mr Darcy?"

"She remains in London."

"What a pity she and her brother will be separated for Christmas."

"Actually, I think them both rather grateful for it," Darcy muttered. When Elizabeth's eyebrows shot still further up her forehead at this wry acknowledgement, he hastened to explain. "Miss Bingley is fond of London society and relishes the opportunity to socialise and be seen, particularly at Christmas."

"You and Mr Bingley do not share her desire?" Elizabeth asked, wryly. "*To be seen?*"

"I imagine, if you know me but at all, you would understand how little the notion of such a thing appeals."

The honesty of this answer startled Elizabeth, and she returned Mr Darcy's guileless smile with one of her own.

"In this, it appears we share a common interest, Mr Darcy. I would much rather spend Christmas surrounded by my family and able to quietly enjoy the comforts of the season than being forced to attend a vast array of society parties."

"Then I hope you will not think our presence intended to interrupt such familial felicity," Mr Darcy said, with a brief bow.

There was a movement by the door that interrupted Elizabeth before she could speak again, and all heads turned to see Jane enter, a shy smile lighting her features with more warmth and delight than had been evidenced there for quite some time.

"Mr Bingley! Mr Darcy! When Kitty told me of your return I felt certain she was teasing me, and yet here I see she told the truth all along."

Kitty frowned, sniffing back the tears that not being believed had wrought. She flew to her mother, and was patted distractedly on one shoulder, and eventually found comfort in her aunt's corner, where she sat, contentedly watching the rest of the conversations in silence.

"Miss Bennet!" Mr Bingley greeted her with warmth and affection that was plain even to Elizabeth's ears. She darted a glance towards Mr Darcy, and was surprised to see a look of contentment resting over his dark features. He appeared to approve very much of Bingley's smiling attentions to Jane, which was so at odds with the picture Elizabeth had constructed of Mr Darcy's feelings towards the match that she quite lost herself in trying to discern what lay beneath this sudden reversal.

"Is something the matter, Lizzy?" Lydia asked, as she danced back to her own seat, and allowed the tea to be served. "Surely you have seen Mr Darcy before and need not stare at him as if he were a stranger here!"

This was said in a stage-whisper, but it was enough to cause Elizabeth to start, and blush, and look very determinedly away. All of these she did not manage quite quickly enough to avoid Mr Darcy turning his head and looking directly at her in surprise, which made Lydia hiccup with laughter.

"And what are your plans for Christmas, gentlemen?" Mrs Bennet asked, fully enjoying her role as host to such a lively party.

"We are for Netherfield!" Bingley said. "Where we shall pass a very quiet Christmas indeed, for it shall be nought but the two of us - and Georgiana, God-willing."

"Your sister hopes to join you?" Elizabeth asked. The mention of Georgiana provoked interest in her, for she had long nursed a desire to be acquainted with the young woman she had heard so many pleasing reports of.

"Yes," Darcy turned towards her, his lips rising in a slight smile. "I do hope you might have cause to become acquainted with her, Miss Elizabeth." Recalling the presence of her sisters, he extended the invitation to all of the young ladies. "That is, I hope she might find friends amongst you. She will know nobody here save for Charles and me and -" he hesitated, shaking his head almost imperceptibly before continuing. "I do not foresee her eager to go to Meryton alone." He turned to Elizabeth again. "I would hope I might entrust her to your care, Miss Elizabeth. I believe she would benefit greatly from such a friendship, and it would be a great personal favour to me to know that my sister had such a kind friend."

Lizzy felt warmth pool in her cheeks to be thus singled out, and nodded, fervently, little trusting herself to utter any words in response to such a request. When Mr Darcy looked at her, she felt her cheeks grow warmer still, so that she was forced to look away. How was it that she, who he had so recently made no attempt to hide his disdain for, was the one young lady present he particularly wished to befriend his sister? *I do not know what spirit overtook you in London, Mr Darcy,* Elizabeth mused, stirring her tea thoughtfully. *But I cannot own I dislike it.*

DARKNESS WAS FALLING by the time Darcy and Bingley arrived at Netherfield. They had been inveigled into spending far longer than either one intended to at Longbourn, a state which neither gentlemen appeared to mind.

Indeed, Darcy was surprised how little he himself had minded it. Instead of being irritated by Mrs Bennet's pestering, he had been touched to note the genuine affection the older woman appeared to display at seeing their neighbours returned so soon to Hertfordshire. Much of her attention had been focused on Bingley, too, which allowed Darcy all the freedom he might wish for in observing the interactions of the other people in the room. Mrs Gardiner had been eager to speak with him again, and he was glad to hear her relate her memories of his father from when she was a girl. That she had done so within Elizabeth's hearing ought to have been a cause for concern, that Elizabeth might think ill of him to enjoy having his father's many virtues thus paraded. Instead, when he had chanced to look at her, he had seen real sympathy in her features for the departed old Mr Darcy, and the impact such a loss had had on his only son.

Indeed, it was in his interactions with Elizabeth that he had been most pleasantly surprised. She had been cautious, at first, but relaxed as the day wore on, so that their conversations evolved from the stilted small talk of strangers to a vast and vivid exchange of feelings on everything from the weather to the latest developments in France, to current trends in books, music, art - in short, he had found her to be as witty and intelligent as his subconscious had intimated her to be, yet in this iteration he had not struggled in keeping up his own end of the conversation. At his mention of Georgiana, she had smiled, and bid him tell her more about his sister, who had up until then been but a name to her. This was easy for Darcy: he was fond of his sister and enjoyed speaking of her virtues, of which there were many. It did him good, too, to dwell on this truer picture of Georgiana than the one his dreams had tormented him with the previous evening. How delighted he would be to behold her again in the flesh and be able to reassure himself, for certain, that she was her own self and not some festive sprite sent to disturb his sleeping self.

"What a fine day!" Bingley declared, as they finished a light supper and retired to the study. Neither gentlemen wished to be too demanding of the staff that were surprised by their return, so they had settled to drinking brandy in a small room that could be easily warmed by a fire and good company.

"It certainly appears to have cheered your spirits," Darcy acknowledged, crossing his legs at the ankle and leaning back in the comfortable chair that he had claimed as his own during his stay at Netherfield.

"Yes, I take no shame in confessing my spirits were a little discontent at being in London," Charles acknowledged, taking a sip of his drink. "I much prefer living in the country, and with such kind neighbours as the Bennets - I really feel we shall have a far better Christmas than anything Caroline might have conjured for us in London." He smiled, recalling some delicate moment of conversation between himself and Jane Bennet earlier that very day. "I think we might ride over there again tomorrow, Darcy, and pay a proper call."

"What was today, if not a proper call?" Darcy asked, nonetheless willing to indulge his friend in this flight of fancy.

"It was an opportunity: but it is not how these things ought really to be done," Bingley mused. "Mr Bennet was not at home, and really -" he paused, straightening a little in his chair and colouring in his cheeks that was not entirely due to his proximity to the fire crackling in the hearth.

"You do not move slowly, do you, Charles?" Darcy acknowledged, with a grin.

"What cause is there to delay?" Charles was philosophical. "You said yourself that Miss Bennet is all that is beautiful and good in the world. It serves me ill to toy with her on account of patience or propriety."

"The first you have not been innately blessed with: the second, I shall recommend you adhere to." Darcy saluted him with his glass, nonetheless happy to see his friend so enthusiastic and contented with his plans.

"Then you will ride over with me?" Charles asked, chewing his lip. "For I confess I do not wish to go alone."

"I hardly think you need me-" Darcy began.

"Oh, but I do. I shall ruin it, I know I shall. What is it one says? *Dearly beloved...*"

"That is the minister," Darcy interjected, drily. "I do not believe the Church of England has yet conceived of a liturgy for the eligible young suitor proposing marriage."

"Of course." Charles grinned, downing his drink in one mouthful with a grimace. "You see? I need you by my side, for Mr Bennet will think me quite stupid and is likely to deny me my opportunity on account of it." Charles' voice dropped. "And I am not stupid, only a little nervous."

"Which state he will no doubt praise you for. It speaks to your good character and the depths of your affections for Miss Bennet." Darcy rose, pouring a drop more brandy into his glass and refilling Charles'. "If you wish me there, of course, I will come."

"You are a good friend, Darcy." Charles yawned. "And now that that is settled, I think I shall retire." He set his glass down, scarcely noticing it still contained some brandy.

Darcy bid him goodnight but lingered a while in the warm glow of the fire. He was not surprised to see Bingley so intent on declaring his feelings to Jane and securing her hand in marriage so soon. In fact, he rejoiced at it. He had successfully routed one part of his dream, thus he could feel satisfied the rest would fade like smoke as well. He shook his head, marvelling at the power such images had held over him. Still, now, in the shadows cast by the fire against the wall, he could recall every emotion that had plagued him in his dreams. *What nonsense*, he thought, sleepily swallowing the last of his draught and feeling his eyelids grow heavy. *Surely I am the only adult in all England so tormented by figments of my own imagination!*

Chapter Thirteen

Elizabeth Bennet bolted upright in bed, her heart hammering in her chest. She glanced around the familiar room, watching the interplay of shadows over the quilt that had been hers for as long as she could remember, and allowed her breathing to return to normal.

How ridiculous! she thought, smiling to herself at the shock of waking so suddenly from her dream and needing to reassure herself so carefully that it had been exactly that: a dream, not real life at all.

For it had *felt* like real life: her life. The vaguest feeling of disappointment settled over her, and she slid back down into her bed, pulling the blankets up to her chin. She had been married, which was in and of itself not so strange a dream. She might not cling so fervently to romance as either Jane or Lydia, in their differing ways, but she had nursed her own dreams of love and marriage, had lived a hundred different romances in the novels she had read. But this dream had not been sweeping in scope, nor disproportionately thrilling and adventurous. It had, in fact, been a very ordinary sort of a dream. She toured a grand house, her house, although it was not one she could recall ever seeing before and was far grander than either Longbourn or Netherfield, which she might have expected after a day spent discussing both houses and their occupants in detail.

And that is the explanation for Mr Darcy's presence in my dream, I am sure! Lizzy thought, stifling a laugh. For she had been married to him, in this alternate version of real life. He had been just the same as ever he was, although he smiled rather more readily in her imagination than he seemed to in real life, and although they had squabbled and teased one another, it had been with smiles and affection and made into a game. A game! As if she could ever imagine Mr Darcy possessing such a sense of humour.

And yet...his reappearance that afternoon had surprised her. He had been the same Mr Darcy she had known at Meryton and Netherfield, and yet he had been changed. His manner was warmer, his frown less fierce. At the mention of his sister, in fact, he had been almost cheerful.

A line of melody tugged at Elizabeth's memory and she tried and failed to catch hold of it. There had been a notion of Georgiana in her dream too, playing the piano somewhere in the distance. That must have been down to Mr Darcy's description of her that afternoon. Lizzy had protested that whilst she would try her best to make Georgiana feel welcome, she worried that the poor girl would suffer if she imagined Elizabeth to be musical, for, whilst she appreciated talent and enjoyed listening to music, she did not possess any amount of natural skill. Mr Bingley had laughed, and declared that *Georgiana Darcy possesses enough natural skill at the pianoforte for half a dozen women combined*, which had made Mama momentarily fret, before she realised there was no hidden slight against any one of her daughters contained within these words, and she declared that she, too, looked forward to hearing Miss Georgiana play sometime during her stay.

Elizabeth rolled over, burying her face in her pillow. It was a nonsense dream, constructed from snatches of remembered conversation, nothing more. Yet it had not been unpleasant to be married to Mr Darcy, even if only in a dream.

Jane's romance is catching, she thought, wryly recalling Jane's whispered excitement about being reunited with Mr Bingley. The two girls had sat up late after their sisters and parents had retired to bed discussing precisely what Mr Bingley had meant when he promised to call the next day and speak to Mr Bennet. Jane had downplayed the notion that he wished to speak of marriage, but Lizzy remained convinced that was the case.

A few hours more and one of us will be proved correct in our assumptions, she thought, lifting her head from the pillow and peering towards the window. She wondered, idly, if Mr Bingley would come alone to see Father, or if Mr Darcy would accompany him. She was succumbing to sleep once more before she could address why such a thing should matter to her...

Chapter Fourteen

Darcy could not put into words his relief at reaching Longbourn the next day. It was not so much for his own sake that he was relieved, but for Charles. His friend had barely sat still for a minute all morning and seemed to be in such a high state of agitation that Darcy was almost poised to take the matter out of his hands and demand an answer to the question himself if only to ensure it was asked expediently.

"Good morning, Mrs Bennet. I wonder if your husband is at home?" he asked, speaking where his friend could not. Upon their arrival at Longbourn, Darcy had expected a repeat of the previous day but was surprised - and somewhat delighted - to see the house's occupants reduced by half.

"He is in his study," Mrs Bennet said, beaming first at Darcy, then Charles. "But please, gentlemen, do come and take tea with us in the sitting room and he will join us very shortly." She turned away, the very model of politeness shattering with the volume with which she summoned her husband. "Mr Bennet!" she screeched. "They are here! You must not keep them waiting!"

Her referral to a nameless *them* suggested to Darcy that both he and his friend had been discussed in their absence, and their call this morning was not only expected, it had been eagerly anticipated, at least by Mrs Bennet. Drawing a breath, he followed his friend into the sitting room, surprised to see but two of the five Bennet daughters there.

"Good morning Miss Bennet. Miss Elizabeth."

Duty satisfied, he selected a seat and gratefully sank into it.

"Where is everyone this morning?" Charles asked, finding his voice at last. "Darcy and I expected a party."

"Alas, you have missed it, in that case," Elizabeth remarked, stifling a yawn. "My aunt and uncle have taken Mary, Lydia and Kitty into Meryton for the day." She blinked, and smiled at Jane. "Although we shall be sure to tell them they were missed."

"I am surprised you did not go with them, Miss Elizabeth, for I believed you fond of walking above all else," Darcy observed.

"Had I gone, I would have been disappointed, in that case," she said, meeting his eyes. She coloured, slightly, and dropped her gaze. "For they have taken a carriage."

Darcy was surprised to see the normally adroit Elizabeth apparently uneasy and was poised to enquire after her health. He noticed dark circles under her eyes and was momentarily concerned that she was unwell, but before he could say a word, Mr Bennet appeared in the doorway.

"Good morning gentlemen!" he said, cheerfully greeting the new arrivals. "Now, which of you wished to speak to me?" He raised his eyebrows. "My wife has scarcely let me forget that I had a meeting of the utmost importance before me this morning. Do, please, let us embark upon it so that the house may return to its common state of peace."

Charles hesitated a moment, before standing, and smiling sheepishly about the room. He followed Mr Bennet back into his study, and Mrs Bennet fluttered anxiously in the doorway, before mumbling some excuse and hurrying after her husband where, Darcy imagined, she would be pressing herself against the study door and straining to hear all that was said within.

Jane glanced, worriedly, at her sister, and the exchange was not missed by Darcy, who cleared his throat.

"I believe it will be good news, Miss Bennet, if my friend's state of nervous agitation is anything to go by."

"Good news for whom?" Elizabeth asked, with an arch smile.

"I imagine that depends on your father, Miss Elizabeth," he remarked. "What results from my friend's proposal is entirely out of my hands now."

"Now?"

"As it should ever have been." Darcy turned directly to Jane, bowing his head. "I apologise for any difficulty my concern for my friend may have caused you." He returned his gaze to Elizabeth. "To either of you."

This was uttered so quickly and simply that it surprised even Darcy. Feel it as he might, he had certainly never intended on uttering such an apology within either of the Miss Bennets' hearing. Elizabeth's reaction made his words worth it, though, and he was gratified to see her surprise soften into a smile, which he returned, forgetting for half a moment that there was anybody else in the room besides the two of them.

A shriek from Mrs Bennet abruptly shattered the illusion, as she came running back into the sitting room, tugging a startled Bingley after her.

"There! There, Mr Bingley, you may tell Jane your news." She shoved him towards Jane, who blushed, and stood, wringing her hands expectantly.

"Mama!" Elizabeth was next to her feet. "Honestly, you are ridiculous. Mr Bingley, don't say a word. We might at least afford you some privacy." She glanced over towards Darcy, who obediently stood, and bowed, briefly, towards Jane and his friend, and followed Elizabeth out into the hallway. Mrs Bennet took rather more persuading to leave the couple a moment or two to themselves, that Bingley might inquire whether Jane's feelings remained unchanged, as his most evidently did.

"Isn't it wonderful?" Mrs Bingley clutched her hands to her ample bosom and sighed rapturously. "What a perfect Christmas gift!"

"Jane has not said yes, yet, Mama."

Mrs Bennet turned towards Elizabeth with a worried glance.

"Oh! You do not think -"

"Not for a moment," Elizabeth said, patting her mother gently on the arm. She glanced around the crowded corridor. "But I think, if it is alright with you, I might take a turn about the gardens."

Darcy immediately latched onto the least traumatic of the two options open to him for his immediate occupation.

"Allow me to accompany you, Miss Elizabeth." The thought of being alone with her might cause his heart to pound somewhat uncomfortably in his chest, and at such a volume that he was certain it was distinguishable by everybody present, but he at least would prefer it to being cooped up with a desperate Mrs Bennet, who would no doubt turn her attentions to him next.

They walked a few steps in silence, both shivering slightly at the sudden change in temperature.

"You do not share your mother's excitement about the promise of a wedding." It was a statement, rather than a question, but nonetheless, Elizabeth turned to answer it.

"I do not share my mother's *exhibition* of excitement," she corrected him. "But I am delighted that my sister will be happy. And Mr Bingley, too." She cast an arch glance at Mr Darcy. "I am surprised to see you pitched in favour of the match, for I felt certain you did not approve."

"I did not," Darcy admitted. "But as I said before, I have changed my mind." He frowned. "Or do you not believe a man capable of such a thing?"

"*A man*, yes," Elizabeth allowed. "I was less convinced of *your* ability to change." She coloured, and ducked her head. "So perhaps I must repent of past positions, also." She smiled, her eyes dancing with good humour. "What strange effects Christmas is wreaking over us both, Mr Darcy. Do not you feel something strange in the air?"

Darcy shivered, folding his hands into fists.

"I certainly feel something *cold* in the air. Tell me, do you think it possible that even my chatterbox friend has finished uttering his proposal by now, that we might return to the fire?"

Elizabeth smirked.

"I am quite sure he has. Whether my mother has let him go from her embrace is another question. Still, at least she will be utterly distracted by him and Jane for the foreseeable future.

You might consider yourself safe, Mr Darcy, at least for the present."

THE REJOICING AT LONGBOURN was scarcely ceased when both Mr Darcy and Mr Bingley took their leave. Indeed, they were only permitted to part when Mr Bingley had uttered an excitable invitation to the Longbourn party to join them at Netherfield for dinner that very evening.

"With Darcy's sister we shall be an extended family indeed!" he had said, his eyes bright. When Mrs Bennet mentioned in passing the absence of his sister, Bingley had blinked, as if recalling quite by chance that Caroline was not there.

"She will be there in spirit, I am sure," Elizabeth had put in, and the momentary silence had been roundly got over.

Longbourn itself had been taken over by a spirit of joy all day, so that Elizabeth was barely permitted a moment alone with Jane until she stole her sister away to "ready themselves for the evening", which mean dismissing Jane as "perfectly lovely" and working to wrestle her own dark curls into submission, whilst quizzing her sister on every detail of Mr Bingley's proposal.

"I am so happy for you, Jane!" She sighed, turning away from the mirror, at last, to regard the figure of her sister, sitting primly on the edge of Lizzy's bed.

"I think I am happy for myself, too," Jane admitted, with a self-deprecating laugh. "Although I can scarcely credit it to be true. To think, Lizzy, just a few days ago we were convinced we would never see Mr Bingley or Mr Darcy again, and now here they are returned to us just in time for Christmas!"

"Indeed," Lizzy mused, recalling how changed at least one of those gentlemen seemed to have been by their short trip away. She felt as if she and Mr Darcy had spoken more to one another in the past twenty-four hours than in the entirety of their acquaintance, and she was still more surprised to find herself enjoying their interactions. His scowl, which she had become so inured to as to consider it his true face, had faded and been replaced by an openness of manner and feature that was almost...handsome.

"What are you thinking about, Lizzy?" Jane asked, tossing a hair-ribbon towards her. "I have every excuse to be vacant at present, for my mind is already turning with notions of weddings and where Mr Bingley and I might make our home once we are wed." She blushed, prettily, as she uttered the word. "But what is your excuse?" Her happy countenance faded. "You do not regret the match?"

"Regret it?" Lizzy laughed. "Hardly! I only regret how long it took you to reach an agreement, for if I had had my way, you would have been wed after your first dance." She shrugged her shoulders. "I own that Providence perhaps knew better."

"Providence or Mr Darcy," Jane remarked, carelessly. "Do you know, Lizzy, it was at his insistence that the pair returned so speedily to Hertfordshire? Charles - that is, Mr Bingley - credits him entirely with hastening to Longbourn that we might settle the matter just as soon as we could. Do not you think that most kind of him?"

"Most kind," Lizzy agreed, adding this detail to her newly-transformed mental picture of Mr Darcy.

"Apparently he, too, was eager to return to Hertfordshire, despite having his own house in London where he might comfortably wait out the season in solitude, should he have wished it. Bingley reckons on some strange occurrences in Darcy's mind over the past few days." She shook her head. "He spoke of a night of restlessness, bad dreams that propelled Darcy to change. Is that not strange? I thought Mr Darcy an utterly logical man, unshaken by mere imaginings."

Elizabeth laughed, but she was reminded of her own nightly imaginings the previous evening. She would always have said the same was true of herself: that she was too sensible to allow herself to be swept away in dreaming, and yet she had been unable to rid Mr Darcy from her mind, and in fact, had found herself strangely shy around him all day, as if her dream had permitted her to see a side of their neighbour that she had not heretofore known existed, let alone appreciated. Perhaps he was not different at all: it was merely that she was able to see what he previously kept hidden.

"There! You are lost to me again!" Jane chided, with a musical laugh. "I know you said you slept poorly last night, Lizzy. Are you well enough to come to dinner this evening? Whilst you would be missed, I am sure everyone would understand if you prefer to rest..."

"No!" Lizzy said, with an urgency that surprised her. "No," she softened her voice. "I am eager to go, Jane, and see you at pride of place with your husband-to-be." She linked her arm through Jane's and the two girls began to descend the stairs. "In any case, I am excited to see Mr Darcy's sister, Georgiana. I have promised to be her friend, and you must help me, Jane, if she is as stern as he is wont to be."

As she said the words she felt their untruth and frowned.

"Although, I wager you are right, for he has not seemed half so stern to me of late as he did before their party departed for London. Perhaps we must rejoice in whatever bad dreams prompted Mr Darcy's return, for they have sent him back to us a changed man. A far pleasanter one, at that."

"Far pleasanter," Jane agreed, but she shot her sister a surprised, amused look that Elizabeth chose not to notice.

"Girls!" Mrs Bennet heralded them from the front doorway. "Are you ready at last? We are going to be late. Where is Lydia? Oh, Kitty, dear! You cannot possibly wish to wear all that lace. This is only an informal dinner after all. Come here -"

Lizzy let go of Jane's arm, for her sister wished to speak a word with their father, and sidestepped the rest of her family for the door, making her way alone towards the carriage. Her mind was still on Mr Darcy, and she felt her heart speed up at the thought of the evening ahead of them. She was excited to meet the famed Georgiana, as she had confessed to Jane, but she was perhaps even more excited to be reunited with Mr Darcy himself. She bit her lip. How strange it was to feel so differently about a man she had previously counselled herself to dislike. She pinched herself, hard, on the forearm, to determine she was not still in her dream-world of the night before.

"Ouch!" she exclaimed aloud, and rubbed at the offending pinch, fearing it would bruise before the evening was out. She coloured at her silliness, and the warmth remained in her cheeks. It was not a dream, then. She could not blame her excitement to see Mr Darcy on anything other than her own real feelings.

She was glad when her sisters began to pile into the carriage after her, for their excited chatter prohibited any further dwelling on her thoughts or feelings, and she determined to do her best to ignore them and enjoy the evening without worrying.

Chapter Fifteen

Georgiana had barely been still for a quarter of an hour altogether. Since arriving at Netherfield, she had embraced her brother, rejoiced with Charles Bingley at the news of his engagement and hurried to bring Darcy up to date on all the happenings at Rosings. Lady Catherine was, by all accounts, rather disappointed that her curate had been seemingly spurned by the Bennets, who must think very highly of themselves indeed to spurn such a practical match. Still, the newly arrived Mrs Collins - nee Lucas - was proving herself amiable and useful and utterly redeemed her husband, which person Georgiana did not greatly esteem.

"He made such a funny figure, William, that I could scarcely attend to all he said, I was struggling so hard to maintain my composure and not betray myself by laughing at his continuous sermonizing." She smiled, bowing her head contritely. "Still, he appeared to think very highly of you and by extension, I think I endeared myself to him as well. And he did not speak too unkindly of his "spirited cousin Elizabeth", though I wager his opinion was tempered by his wife, for I believe it to be true that Charlotte Collins is a great friend of Miss Elizabeth's."

Here, Georgiana, at last, paused for breath, fixing her attention squarely on her brother, so that Darcy was forced to offer a disinterested "Hmmm" in response. The appearance of disinterest, anyway, for he found his ears pricked up at every mention Georgiana made of Elizabeth, though the two young women were at present nought but names to one another.

"I was surprised to hear of your return to Hertfordshire, brother, and still more by your summoning me here for Christmas."

Darcy frowned and Georgiana hurried to placate him

"Oh, do not misunderstand me, William. I am delighted to be here, for I have not seen enough of you since - since Ramsgate." Georgiana's happy manner faltered a fraction and he reached his hand out, resting it gently on Georgiana's clenched fists.

"We needn't talk of it, Georgiana, unless you wish to." His lips quirked. "Not to me, either. I am sure you will find a firm friend in Miss Bennet. That is, Miss Elizabeth. Should you wish to discuss the matter with one more inclined to understand your feminine sensibilities..." he trailed off, feeling inordinately aware of the curious stare his sister had fixed upon him.

"That is the third time you have mentioned Miss Elizabeth in the past quarter hour," she observed, with a knowing smile.

"Is it?" Darcy shrugged. "If she has been a feature of our conversation it is likely because you sought to mention her after your meeting with Mr Collins. There can be no other reason."

"Indeed." Georgiana laughed. "Well, I shall turn your words back upon you, brother, and declare there is no need for us to discuss it further. Come! Do permit me to see the house a little more before your friends arrive. I would ask Mr Bingley for a tour but he looks so out of his depth in arranging the particulars of our dinner that I could not dream of adding to his anxieties." She slid her arm through the crook of Darcy's and drew him to his feet.

The pair were making their way back downstairs when Georgiana discerned the sound of a carriage approaching and pushed Darcy forward.

"They're here!"

"Apparently," Darcy remarked, with an irritable smile at the sudden fit of shyness that prompted his sister to hide, ineffectually, behind him as the door flew open to admit Mr and Mrs Gardiner, Mr and Mrs Bennet and the five young ladies.

"Mr Darcy!" Mrs Bennet cooed, her previous dislike of him utterly remedied by what she perceived to be his direct intervention in Bingley's proposal to Jane. "Who is that hiding behind you? Why, this must be the famous sister we have heard so much about. Step into the light, dearie, and be introduced to us. We shan't bite!"

"Unless you annoy us greatly," Mr Bennet said with a smile. "Come, my dear Mrs Bennet and let us go into the sitting room. I hardly think stairwells and corridors the best place for new acquaintances."

Mr Bingley's appearance in the doorway of the parlour captured Mrs Bennet's attention and she flounced in that direction on her husband's arm. Taking a deep breath, Georgiana stepped forward and was met with a warm smile by Elizabeth.

"You must be Georgiana," she said, her eyes travelling momentarily to Mr Darcy's and then back to his sister. "You must not mind Mama," she lowered her voice to a whisper. "She is harmless, or relatively so. Particularly if you are not a wealthy man in need of a wife, would not you say, Mr Darcy?"

"I can scarcely comment," he replied, but a rogue smirk belied his polite response and he was rewarded with a smile from Elizabeth, who stepped forward and walked with Georgiana.

"When did you arrive?"

"This afternoon, Miss Elizabeth."

"Oh, call me Lizzy!" Elizabeth said, warmly. "For I have it on good authority that we are going to be great friends."

"Very well, Lizzy." Georgiana's features brightened at the instruction and Darcy was pleased to see the two young ladies he most respected finding a friendship he himself had hoped for.

How is it I only now recognise your kindness, Elizabeth? he silently asked her back, as they walked into the sitting room. *Your kindness, your humour, your warmth. How glad I am to see you care for my sister so readily, as I hoped you would. I only wish you might one day grant me the same permission to call you not "Elizabeth" but Lizzy, and not "Miss Bennet" but something else altogether.* His lips quirked, at the name that flitted through his brain as fleetingly as a wisp of smoke. *"Mrs Darcy."*

AFTER A JOYFUL, FESTIVE meal, filled with good food and neighbourly conversation, everyone retired back to the parlour, where Georgiana was pressed into playing for everyone a selection of Christmas carols. She had won over almost everybody by her skill and self-deprecation: and then proceeded to win even Mary Bennet to her side by suggesting the two play a few songs as duets. This had the effect of drawing Kitty and Lydia into the musical corner, too, as they sought to exhibit their vocal skills and a pretty little chorus came together under Georgiana's generous tutelage.

"You see, Mr Darcy? Your concerns for your sister were quite unfounded," she whispered, as she found herself beside Mr Darcy in a quiet corner of the sitting room.

"It was your greeting that gave her the confidence to befriend your sisters," he replied. "And for that I am grateful. She can be reserved -"

"Like her brother," Elizabeth put in, fearing he had taken her joke for a slight, as his features rearranged themselves slowly but firmly into a smile.

"Yes, like her brother. I assure you that is about the only way in which we are alike. Georgiana far outstrips me in amiability and optimism."

Lizzy laughed.

"Well, we certainly cannot accuse you of self-deception, Mr Darcy."

"Now *that* I cannot allow. Until quite recently I would argue I was quite adept at deceiving myself." Colour swept across his cheeks, but Lizzy, emboldened by their growing ease of manner, pressed him to answer.

"I cannot believe it. Mr Darcy, untrue?"

"Mistaken, not untrue - or, not knowingly untrue."

"And what have you been mistaken about?"

"The first I already alluded to: the nature of the affection between my friend and your sister. I have repented and, I hope, helped to undo any damage I in any way contributed to." Lizzy nodded, but said nothing, allowing him to continue which, after a pause, he did.

"The second, I confess now, though I wonder at my doing so." Darcy's voice had dropped to barely a whisper and when Lizzy glanced at him the look he fixed on her was so serious, so striking that she felt, rather than heard, his response.

"It is you, Miss Elizabeth. I was mistaken in my opinion of you and I deceived myself, for far longer than is admirable, of my indifference."

"Then you are not...indifferent?" Lizzy's throat was dry. For one brief, terrifying moment she feared his answer would be worse. She pictured him saying *I am not indifferent, in fact, I despise you.* She shook off the notion when she felt his gaze once more and saw the ghost of a smile resting on his stormy features. It was a smile she recognised and served to settle her nerves.

"When we went to London it was to spirit Charles away from Miss Bennet: that much I have confessed to. What I have not said was that it was also my own attempt to escape from you. At that, I was still more unsuccessful, for you followed me there."

Lizzy frowned, opening her mouth to say in no uncertain terms that she had not left Hertfordshire, nor been anywhere close to London this past year.

"Oh, not in person," Darcy acknowledged. He grimaced, but it was an amusing, self-deprecating expression, utterly different to the proud disapproval he had so often worn previously.

"You shall think me mad. But it seemed to me I saw you everywhere I looked. You were in the faces of strangers I passed on the street, you haunted my evenings. It was my inner self, I do not doubt, tormenting me with the truth I had not yet had the courage to admit to myself or anyone else. No, Elizabeth," he continued, dropping the "Miss" in his desire to speak earnestly. "I am not indifferent to you."

Lizzy's heart was full as her eyes met his.

"Nor I, you, Mr Darcy."

"I think it entirely possible I may care for you, and I can only hope the thought is not too dreadful-"

Lizzy reached out one hand to stop him from saying more.

"It is not dreadful, Mr Darcy. Not dreadful at all. It is -" she smiled, grateful that the shadows concealed her blush. "It is the very thing I dreamed of."

Epilogue

"Well, this has been a very merry Christmas indeed!" Mr Bennet smiled benevolently over the dining table at Longbourn.

"Indeed it has, Mr Bennet!" his wife announced, beaming at the five young folk who sat together and garnered most of her interest. Darcy had not intended to sit as close as he was to Elizabeth, but could not help but be grateful to Georgiana, who had determined she wished to sit with Miss Elizabeth on one side and her brother on the other, and would not be argued with, on this of all days.

"I had such a peculiar dream last night!" she declared, after Mrs Gardiner had paid her sister-in-law a particular compliment upon the serving of their dinner, and thus captured Mrs Bennet's attention away from their small party.

"Oh dear, are you not comfortable at Netherfield?" Jane asked, with a sympathetic frown.

"Very comfortable!" Georgiana replied. "It was mere imagination that kept me awake, I am sure partly due to my excitement at spending Christmas here, amongst such friends as yourself." She smiled at Jane, and Darcy felt a warmth in his chest at the way his sister had so taken to their neighbours, and how thoroughly she had been welcomed into their circle.

"Well, Georgiana, does the dream bear repeating?" Charles asked, with a grin. "What nonsense forced you into wakefulness at so early an hour?"

"It was not nonsense!" Georgiana protested. She could barely contain a smile and Darcy felt his suspicions rise as she cast a sly glance at him. "In fact, brother, you were its chief character."

"Oh dear. I am quite sure I do not wish to hear it, in that case!"

"No, you must, for I am sure you shall find it as amusing as I do, upon reflection." Georgiana set her cup down, surveying her friends until she was sure she captured their whole attention. "For I dreamed you were married."

"Married?" Charles exclaimed. "Darcy?"

Darcy concentrated on remaining nonchalant, but even then he could not prevent his gaze from straying towards Elizabeth, who was taking particular interest in the remnants of her plum pudding.

"Do you not care to ask to whom?"

"It seems you care to tell me, sister."

"It was to Miss Elizabeth!" Georgiana clapped her hands. "You were married, and living at Pemberley. It made for a delightful picture."

"Delightful?" Lydia Bennet had angled her ear towards their corner of the table in time enough to hear this pronouncement. She snorted with laughter. "Mr Darcy and *Elizabeth?* I wonder at your calling it a dream, Georgie dear. Surely it was a nightmare!"

Darcy frowned, turning to set the young Miss Lydia straight, until he felt a hand on his shoulder, and realised Elizabeth stood behind him.

"Actually, Lydia, Georgiana's dream may have been fiction but it need not remain so." Her voice faltered a little, and Darcy rose to his feet, taking on the challenge of speaking.

"Mr and Mrs Bennet, Mr and Mrs Gardiner." He cleared his throat. "It was not my intention to raise this matter on Christmas day - or at the dinner table - but it seems providence, or my sister, had another notion in mind."

"Is something the matter, Mr Darcy?" Mr Bennet asked.

"It is merely the matter of confessing to you that I wish to marry your daughter, Elizabeth."

Mrs Bennet's cutlery clattered noisily to her plate.

"Lizzy?" she squeaked. "You wish to marry *Lizzy?*"

"I do." Darcy warmed to his topic as he spoke. "*We* do."

"How did you decide this?" Mrs Bennet wailed. "When?"

"I would imagine it was when you arrived back from London and saw us by the road, Mr Darcy, or sometime near then?" Mrs Gardiner's eyes sparkled with fun, and not a glimmer of surprise. "Why else would you be so eager to return straight away to Hertfordshire?"

Darcy had no answer to give, but fortunately at that moment, Georgiana let out a delighted laugh and silenced any need for further words.

"My dream will come true, in that case. And here I thought dreams were of such little consequence as to be scarcely worth remarking upon!"

Darcy turned back to Elizabeth, gathering her hands in his.

"I would not say that, Georgiana. I think in dreams we often see things far more plainly than we might manage in wakefulness, if only we have the courage to act on what we see…"

"Two daughters to wed in the new year!" Mrs Bennet hissed, in a voice that was neither quiet nor subtle. "And to think, Mr Bennet, you declared that this Christmas would be a very dull affair. How wrong you have been! I could never have dreamed of a better!"

The End

Also by Meg Osborne

A Convenient Marriage
Longbourn's Lark: A Pride and Prejudice Variation
Three Weeks in Kent: A Pride and Prejudice Variation
Suitably Wed: A Pride and Prejudice Variation

Fate and Fortune
Too Fond of Stars: A Persuasion Variation
A Temporary Peace: A Persuasion Variation

Love Remains
Reacquainted
Rediscovered
Reunited
Love Remains Omnibus

Pathway to Pemberley

The Collins Conundrum: A Pride and Prejudice Variation
The Wickham Wager: A Pride and Prejudice Variation
The Darcy Decision: A Pride and Prejudice Variation

Standalone
After the Letter: A Persuasion Continuation
Half the Sum of Attraction: A Persuasion Prequel
A Very Merry Masquerade: A Pride and Prejudice Variation Novella
The Other Elizabeth Bennet: A Pride and Prejudice Variation Novella
In Netherfield Library and Other Stories
Mr Darcy's Christmas Carol: A Pride and Prejudice Variation

Watch for more at www.megosbornewrites.com.

About the Author

Meg Osborne is an avid reader, tea drinker and unrepentant history nerd. She writes sweet historical romance stories and Jane Austen fanfiction, and can usually be found knitting, dreaming up new stories, or on twitter @megoswrites

Read more at www.megosbornewrites.com.

Printed in Great Britain
by Amazon